PRAISE FOR RELEASE

"Patrick Ness has written a pacy, convincing, coming-of-age novel… Adam's story alone is thrilling, intimate, important, joyous."
THE TIMES

"Passionate and disturbing… A richly layered tale of finding your true family and knowing when to give up on ideals."
OBSERVER

"Every sentence in this gorgeous little novel feels perfect and necessary… This focused, humane book is a joy."
THE NEW YORK TIMES

"Spellbinding… A captivating and emotional tale."
ATTITUDE MAGAZINE

"One of the finest YA novels to have emerged this year."
IRISH TIMES

"Literary, illuminating, and stunningly told."
KIRKUS REVIEWS

"It's frequently gut-wrenching, yet funny, tender and warm."
SUNDAY HERALD

"Ness's great achievement in *Release* is to acknowledge the weight, worth and agony of first love, and to show the richer blooming of a second… It's a book that will speak, with passionate warmth, to anyone who has ever been made to feel 'less than'."
GUARDIAN

RELEASE

PATRICK
NESS

First published 2017 by Walker Books Ltd
87 Vauxhall Walk, London SE11 5HJ

This edition published 2018

2 4 6 8 10 9 7 5 3 1

Text © 2017 Patrick Ness
Cover illustration © 2017 Levente Szabo

"Glacier" (written by John Grant). Published by Blue Mountain Music Ltd/
Showpony Music Ltd. All Rights Reserved. Used By Permission.
All rights administered by Blue Mountain Music Ltd.

This book has been typeset in Sabon and Futura

Printed and bound by CPI Group (UK) Ltd, Croydon CR0 4YY

British Library Cataloguing in Publication Data:
a catalogue record for this book is available from the British Library

ISBN 978-1-4063-7869-6

www.walker.co.uk

MIX
Paper from
responsible sources
FSC® C020471

For John Mullins
1966–2015
Sorely missed

Then (she had felt it only this morning) there was the terror; the overwhelming incapacity, one's parents giving it into one's hands, this life, to be lived to the end, to be walked with serenely; there was in the depths of her heart an awful fear.

–Virginia Woolf, *Mrs Dalloway*

This pain
It is a glacier moving through you
And carving out deep valleys
And creating spectacular landscapes

–John Grant, *Glacier*

1

THE YOKE

Adam would have to get the flowers himself.

His mom had enough to do, she said; she needed them this morning, pretty much *right now* if the day wasn't going to be a total loss; and in the end, Adam's attendance at this little "get-together" with his friends tonight may or may not hinge on his willingness/success in picking up the flowers and doing so without complaint.

Adam argued – quite well, he thought, without showing any overt anger – that his older brother, Marty, was the one who'd run over the *old* flowers; that he, Adam, *also* had a ton of things to do today; and that new chrysanthemums for the front path weren't exactly high in the logical criteria for attendance at a get-together he'd already bargained for – because nothing was free with his parents, not ever – by chopping all the winter's firewood before even the end of August. Nevertheless, she had, in that way of hers, turned it into a decree: he would get the flowers or he wouldn't go tonight, especially after that girl got killed.

"Your choice," his mom said, not even looking at him.

It's only the Yoke, Adam thought, getting behind the wheel of his car. And the Yoke isn't forever. Still, he needed a few deep breaths before he started the engine.

At least it was early. The late summer Saturday stretched ahead, with its hours to fill, hours he *had* filled with a schedule of things (he was a scheduler): he needed to go for a run; he had a few hours' stock-taking to do at the Evil International Mega-Conglomerate; he had to help his dad at the church; he had to stop by Angela's work to make sure the pizzas were still on schedule for the party–

Morning, his phone buzzed in his lap.

He smiled in a small way. There was that today, too.

Morning, he typed back. *Wanna buy flowers?*

Is that code?

He smiled again and backed out of the driveway. Fine, let go of the anger, because what a day ahead! What fun it promised! What laughs! What drinks and food and friends and sex! What a stab in the heart at the end of it because the party was a going-away one! Someone was going away. Adam wasn't sure whether he wanted them to go away or not.

What a day ahead.

What time are you coming by? asked his phone.

Around 2? he typed back at a stop sign.

The reply was a thumbs-up emoji.

He pulled out of his wooded neighbourhood onto the wooded road into town. "Wooded" in fact described everything within fifty miles; it was the overwhelming feature of the town of Frome, indeed the overwhelming feature of the state of Washington. Take it as a given, a sight so often seen it became invisible.

Adam thought about two o'clock this afternoon. There was so much happiness to be had there. So much secret happiness.

And yet, a sinking of the stomach, too…

No, stop that. He was looking forward to it. Absolutely. Yes. In fact, think about–

In fact, yes, *that*.

Another stop sign. *Blood is flowing places*, he messaged. *Engorging things*.

The reply was two thumbs-up emojis.

So consider Adam Thorn, as he pulls out onto the further main road – wooded, naturally – the one that leads to the garden centre, the one with ever-increasing traffic, even at this early hour on a Saturday. Adam Thorn, born almost but not quite eighteen years ago in the hospital ten miles along this same road. The furthest from here he's been in his life is when his family went on a fun-free driving holiday to Mount Rushmore. He didn't even get to go on the mission trip to Uruguay with his father, mother and Marty when Adam was in the sixth grade. Afterwards, his dad had made it sound like a nightmare of mud and evangelical-resistant locals, but Adam – deemed too young and sentenced to three weeks of 4.30 suppers with Grandpa John and Grandma Pat – couldn't help but feel that wasn't the point.

Twelve more months, he thought, and the Yoke is off. Senior year started in just over a week.

After that, the sky.

For Adam Thorn wants to get away. Adam Thorn longs to leave, with an ache in his gut so acute it feels like vertigo. Adam Thorn wishes he was going away with the person going away at the end of tonight's going-away party.

Well, maybe he does.

Adam Thorn. Blanched blond, tall, bulky in a way that might be handsome but is only just starting to properly agree with gravity. A-student, fighting for the college of his choice, fighting for college at *all* as the money troubles that are supposed to be passing don't seem to be doing so, not helped by pointless purchases of chrysanthemums because "preachers' houses have to look a certain way", but he is focused on a goal, focused on what will get him the hell out of Frome, Washington.

Adam Thorn, keeper of secrets.

His phone rang as he pulled into the garden centre. "Everyone's up early today," he answered as he parked.

"How many times do I have to tell you I'm not every-one?" Angela grumped.

"*Everyone* is everyone. Whole point of 'everyone'."

"The whole point of everyone is for them to con-stantly do stupid things while we – not everyone – make fun of them for it and feel superior."

"Why are you up?"

"Why else? The chickens."

"The chickens are every reason for everything. They'll rule us one day."

"They rule us now. Why are *you* up?"

"Replacement flowers. For my mom's garden of punishment."

"You are so going to need therapy."

"They don't believe in it. If you can't pray it away, it's not a real problem."

"Your parents. I'm amazed they're letting you go tonight. Especially after Katherine van Leuwen."

Katherine van Leuwen was the girl who was killed, which seemed impossible with a name so strong. She'd gone to Adam's school, a year ahead, but he didn't know her. And okay, so, fine, she *had* been murdered last week at the same lake where the get-together was planned (Adam had never used the word "party" with his parents as that would have closed discussion immediately), but the girl's killer, her much older boyfriend, had been caught, had confessed, and was awaiting sentencing. She had always hung out with the meth heads and it was meth her boyfriend was amped up on when he killed her, raving about – of all things – goats, according to an equally methed witness. Angela, Adam's closest friend, raged against anyone's even slight suggestion that Katherine van Leuwen had brought it on herself.

"You don't know," she'd nearly shout at whoever. "You don't know what her life was like, you don't know what addiction is like. You have no idea what goes on inside another person's head."

That was certainly true, and thank God for that, in the case of Adam's parents.

"They think it's a quote *get-together* with three or four of my friends to say goodbye to Enzo," he said now.

"That sentence is factually true."

"While at the same time omitting much."

"Also true. When pizzas? Because, pizzas."

"I've got a run to do, then work, then I'm seeing Linus at two, and I have to help my dad set up for church tomorrow—"

"Dad and church post-coitus with Linus? You dirty boy."

"I was thinking seven? Then we could go straight to the party."

"Get-together."

"There will be together to get, yes."

"Seven. Good. I need to speak to you."

"About what?"

"Stuff. Don't worry. And now chickens. Because, chickens."

Angela's family had a working farm. She swore they'd adopted her from Korea because it was cheaper than hiring a labourer for the livestock. This wasn't true, even Angela knew it; Mr and Mrs Darlington were unobtrusively decent, always good to Adam, always giving him an implicitly safe place to get away from those parents of his, even if they were too kind to say such a thing out loud.

"When is it that you've got my back again, Adam?" Angela asked, in their usual farewell.

He grinned. "Always. Until the end of the world."

"Oh, yeah. That's right." She hung up.

He got out of his car into the early morning sunshine. The lot was nearly full at a little past eight. Serious gardeners around here, getting ready for the approaching fall. He stopped a minute under the sky, only cleared of trees for the parking lot but still: open sky. He closed his eyes, felt the sun on his eyelids.

He breathed.

The Yoke wasn't even his word. It was Biblical. It was his dad's. Big Brian Thorn. Former professional football player – three seasons as a tight end for the Seahawks before the shoulder surgery – now long-time head preacher at The House Upon The Rock, Frome's second-largest evangelical church. "Until you leave my house," he'd bellowed right into Adam's face, "you are under my Yoke." Adam's car had been taken away for a month that time. For missing curfew by ten minutes.

He breathed again, then went inside for chrysanthemums.

JD McLaren was working the flower department. They had world literature and chemistry together. "Hey, Adam," he said, with his usual plump friendliness.

"Hey, JD," Adam said. "I didn't even know you guys opened this early."

"They saw how many people were lined up at the drive-thru Starbucks at five every morning and thought there was business they were missing out on."

"They're probably right. I need chrysanthemums."

"Bulbs? Wrong time of year to plant those."

"I need the full, blooming flowers. My brother flattened the ones bordering our driveway. My mother had a stroke."

"Oh, my God!"

"She didn't really have a stroke, JD."

"Oh. Okay."

"But I need to procure them or be denied social occasions."

"You mean Enzo's thing tonight?"

"I do. You going?"

"Yeah. I heard there's going to be kegs because his parents are European and don't care if we drink."

"Angela and I are bringing pizzas from her work."

"Better and better. Does it matter what colour chrysanthemums?"

"Probably, but as she didn't specify, I have the chance to blame her if they're wrong."

"I'll get you the most garish."

"And maybe…"

JD waited. Adam couldn't quite meet his eye. "Maybe not the most expensive?"

"Not a problem, Adam," JD said, seriously, and headed off into the massive field of flower pallets. Those were all in dirt, to be planted into your own gardens, but the garden centre had a cooler of cut flowers, too, if you needed a bouquet. Adam wandered over to it, his brain idly moving through the day ahead, coupled with a song he was presently unaware of even humming.

A red rose, alone in its plastic bucket. He reached for it, though it didn't really register in his consciousness until it was in his hands. A single red rose. Could he buy it? Was that something that was okay? That boys did? If it was for a girl, obviously, yes, but if it was for...

He had no rules for this. Which was liberating some of the time because that meant there were none to obey, not even with Linus. But sometimes a guide or history or a long-established literature would have been useful. Could he buy a rose? And give it? How would Linus take it? Did everyone else in the world know the answer except him?

If it was even Linus he gave it to.

He placed the pad of his right thumb onto one of the rose's thorns – which, along with "crown of", was one of the two "jokes" people told about his last name, never making anyone laugh but themselves – and slowly but firmly pressed. It pierced the skin and in the quickness of the drop of blood that flowed there, he saw–

−an entire world, fast as a gasped breath, of trees and green, of water and woods, of a figure that followed in the darkness, of mistakes made, of loss, of grief−

Adam blinked and put his bloody thumb to his lips. It was gone. Like a dream. Like vapour. Leaving behind only a feeling of disquiet and the tang of blood on his tongue.

When JD returned, Adam bought the rose. It was only two bucks.

She wakes, suddenly, to the smell of blood, of roses, as if her heart has been pricked by a thorn. She is drenched. Has she walked up from the water's edge? Has she stepped out of the water itself?

She doesn't know. There was flurry, there was rush, there was release–

And then a snag, as if on that thorn in her heart, a drop of blood pearling itself...

She sits up and the water pours off her like she passed through a waterfall seconds before. But the shore is dry, as shores go, the mud beneath her damp but firm. She runs her palm over it, like she is mystified by it, and maybe she is. It is coarse under her fingertips. She pinches a bit between her thumb and index finger, bringing it to her nose, inhaling deeply. Rich, peaty, the smell of earth, but not the source of the blood scent.

But then why would it be? she thinks, of a sudden. She is surrounded by wild rose bushes, she knows this, she doesn't know how, but she does. She is surrounded by thorns—

And the scent shimmers away, like a voice heard before waking.

She stands, still dripping into the newly formed puddle at her feet. This dress is hers, she thinks. This dress is not hers, she thinks. The contradiction is true. It is patterned floral, light, tasteful, a young woman's dress but either ironically retro or actually from another time.

Do I wear dresses? she thinks.

Yes. No.

There are pockets in the dress, which would seem to mark it out as very old-fashioned, but they're distended, stretched, heavy. She reaches for the weight inside each and pulls out two solid bricks, dense enough to drag her down.

To drown her.

She stares at them for the longest while.

She drops the bricks. They each bounce once on the mud.

"Death is not the end," she speaks aloud.

What? What was that? What does that even mean? She puts a hand over her mouth as if to keep it from speaking again, holding the words in.

A song. It's a song. She feels the tune humming itself in her diaphragm, a melody emerging, words that she knows. A song for funerals, gravesides. Or perhaps one only written to sound so, perhaps done with the same irony that wove this dress.

She closes her eyes against the sun breaking in the

trees. She sees the veins and capillaries on the insides of her eyelids, red as murder.

She breathes.

Then she vomits up more water than her stomach could possibly contain. It is only water, no bile or food, clear in the cataract that rushes from her mouth. She eventually has to kneel from the force of it, until the over-whelmed puddle beneath her opens a channel to the lake.

Finally, there is no more. She pants, gathering herself. When she stands again, her hair, her skin, her dress, are all dry, not a hint of dampness anywhere.

She breathes once again.

"I will find you," she says, and on bare feet, she begins to walk.

Behind the rose bushes, the faun watches her go. After a moment, he follows, worried.

2

RUN

It took at least a mile, sometimes two, before Adam properly relaxed into his run. "Maybe distance running isn't for you," his cross-country coach had said, at first gently, then not, then eventually giving up when Adam kept coming to practice and completing all his runs. He'd never won a single race – the team had never won a single *meet* – and Adam's awkward first ten minutes were undoubtedly part of that, but...

Once he warmed up, once the tension was gone, once the sweat had properly broken and his breathing was rhythmically heavy and every twinge of stiffness and pain from previous workouts had been obliterated by adrenaline and endorphins, when all of that had happened, there was almost nowhere on earth he'd rather be, even on up-and-down back roads with no shoulder or, as now, on the old railroad path too crowded with entitled cyclists or groups of power-walking moms in their pastel tops and self-crimped hair.

For forty-five minutes, or an hour, or an hour and a half, the world was his, and he was alone in it. Blissfully, wonderfully, almost sacredly alone.

Which was good, because the chrysanthemums had gone down badly.

"Did you purposely get the colours of vomit?" his mother asked.

"That's all they had."

"Are you sure? Are you sure that's what you want to say? When I can very easily go down there and check myself?"

He kept his voice level and repeated, "That's all they had."

She relented, grudgingly. "I suppose it *is* late in the season. But couldn't you have tried another flower? One that looks less like ... bodily functions?"

"You asked for chrysanthemums. If I'd gotten anything else, you'd be sending me back there right now and then both of us would have wasted our mornings."

Not to mention money we don't have on flowers when I haven't had a new winter coat in three years, he did not add.

She had waited a moment, then picked up the pallet and took it out front without a word of thank you. Moments later, when he'd changed into his running gear and sprinted past her to start his workout, she was already arm-deep in topsoil at the side of the driveway. She called something out to him, but he had his earbuds turned up loud and was pretty sure he hadn't heard her.

His parents. They hadn't always been this angry/wary/ scared of him. His childhood had been all right, even filled with talk of "blessings" after four years of effort to have a second child had been so literally fruitless they had just given up. As was often the way with these things, Adam was born eight months later.

My Baby, she'd called him. For too long. For too many years. Until it stopped being a phrase of love and started to contain within it an iron weight of instruction. You will never be our equal, they seemed to be telling him, no matter how old you get. Especially when all his little friends growing up were girls. Especially when he never watched the Super Bowl but never missed the Oscars. Especially when he started to seem "a bit gay".

She'd actually said that in front of him at a Wendy's one Sunday night after church. "Do you think he might be *a bit gay*?" she'd asked across the table to his father, as fifteen-year-old Marty looked furiously into his chocolate Frosty and eleven-year-old Adam's face stung as keenly as a slapped sunburn.

All he had done was mention how fun the dance classes sounded that the son of his sixth-grade teacher was taking.

"*No,*" his father said to his mother too quickly, too firmly. "And don't talk like that. Of course he isn't." With his eye on Adam, making clear this was only partly belief and mostly command and one hundred per cent denial of any dance classes.

The subject hadn't come up again, not once, in the intervening six years.

Nobody here was a fool. Not Adam, who had mastered clever Internet searching before his parents knew what a Wi-Fi child lock even *was*. And his mom and dad were both educated people, not even a little bit blind to what the world was like, how it had changed even in Adam's lifetime. But sometimes it felt like change only happened in far-off cities and was having too much fun there to make it out to the suburbs, where the benefit of his parents' education was merely that they smiled and kept mostly quiet about their certainties rather than discarding them.

His father was an evangelical minister, after all. With Adam as a son. Particular denials of reality were going to be necessary for *anyone* in that house.

So no one talked about it, but there had been curfew and sleepover restrictions that Marty hadn't suffered, first in Adam's friendship with Enzo, and only less in his friendship with Linus because they barely knew Linus existed, Angela covering for him to an extent he'd never be able to repay. Church, twice on Sunday, once on Wednesday, was mandatory, of course, and his regular trips to Christian summer camp were more strictly enforced than Marty's, too – though Marty had been only too happy to go. Even Adam's joining of drama club at school was not so subtly resisted until he told them he was also joining the cross-country team.

He crossed mile four at the end of the old railroad path, having to turn sideways to get past five moms pushing five strollers side by side. It was usually at this point in the run that he was no longer arguing with anyone in his head. Oh, well.

Angela loved *her* parents. They were the kind of family that laughed together over dinner. She hadn't had a curfew since fourteen because they trusted her not to get in any trouble. When she'd lost her "full" virginity, as she called it, the experience hadn't been what Angela was expecting and she and her mom had actually talked it over afterwards (though not before Adam and Angela had thoroughly debriefed first).

Adam imagined the look on his dad's face if he'd gone to him the first time after full penetration with Enzo. An elderly man on what appeared to be a home-made bicycle looked up and grinned at Adam's passing laugh.

Adam turned down the path that ran along a stretch of lakefront, across a side bay from where Enzo's party would be tonight. He had only been planning to run six miles, especially with the chrysanthemum delay, but felt like he needed to make it eight, needed to push that little bit further. He had reached the point, that rare point that sometimes happened in a run, where he felt aware of his youth, aware of his *strength*, aware of the temporary immortality granted in these moments of fullest physical exertion. He could run these last four miles forever. He *would* run them forever.

He heard the car horn honking before he was a hundred feet along the path but assumed it couldn't possibly be for him.

His parents had never really liked Enzo but couldn't bring themselves to say so outright. Enzo – Lorenzo Emiliano Garcia – was from Spain. He'd been born there, though he had no memory of it, his parents having found their way to America shortly after his birth and then to the nearly rural commuter town of Frome just before the eighth grade. He had no accent but had a European passport. Actually, having a passport even without the adjective was impressively strange on its own. But it wasn't that he was moving back to Spain after tonight. His mother, an endocrinologist, had taken a job all the way across the country, in Atlanta. Adam's parents were really only letting him go to the get-together out of relief at Enzo vanishing as an influence in their son's life.

The hilarious thing was that it had nothing to do with all the physical stuff they'd shared, all the sex and love (Could Adam call it that? Did *Enzo*? Did he, though?), the intimacy and closeness. If his parents had genuinely suspected any of *that*, he would have been packed off to ex-gay camp faster than a mosquito's blink.

No, they objected because Enzo was Catholic.

He laughed to himself again as he ran. The endorphins were really cooking now.

"Have you been a witness to this boy?" his father would ask. "It's what the Lord wants of us. What He *demands* of us."

"They go to church every Sunday, Dad. I think they've probably got a Lord of their own."

"Don't blaspheme."

"How is that–"

"You can talk him away from the lie of the papacy."

"That's probably what I should start with, huh?"

"Dang it, Adam! All this, this, this *charisma* you have. All this drive–"

"You think I have charisma?" Adam was genuinely astonished.

"You're not like Martin." It sounded like a painful admission. It almost certainly was. "Your brother ... has different blessings, but he's never going to be as effective with words as you." His dad shook his head. "I prayed for a preacher as a son, and God, in His infinite humour, gave me one with all of the faith but none of the talent and another with all of the talent but none of the faith."

"That's a little hard on Marty, don't you–"

"Just be a witness to this boy, son." Adam was astonished (again) to see what seemed to be tears in his father's eyes. "You could be so effective. So, so effective."

Well, Adam had thought to himself, I've had my mouth on his bare skin. That seemed to be effective.

He didn't say that, though.

Mostly, he was confused by the conversation. Not his dad's evangelizing, of course, but that it was the first time in a long time, too long, that his dad had expressed any hope in him. They'd seemed to decide he was the Prodigal Son in waiting and were happy to let that story play out.

Even the endorphins as he crossed mile five weren't enough to make this feel joyous. He pushed himself, ran harder.

He had loved Enzo. *Loved* him. And who cared if it was the love of a fifteen- and then a sixteen-year-old. Why did that make it any less? They were older than those two idiots in *Romeo and Juliet*. Why did everyone no longer a teenager automatically dismiss any feeling you had then? Who *cared* if he'd grow out of it? That didn't make it any less true in those painful and euphoric days when it was happening. The truth was always now, even if you were young. *Especially* if you were young.

He had loved Enzo.

And then Enzo, for reasons Adam could – still – not quite understand, had stopped loving Adam. They became "friends", though how that was supposed to work, Adam also still didn't know. He'd witnessed to Enzo with his love. If he was as charismatically effective as his father seemed to believe, why hadn't that been enough to make Enzo love him back?

"Shit," he said, stopping on the lake path, putting his hands on his knees and just panting–

"Shit," she hears, as she continues through the trees away from the lake, and there it is again, the same pricking on her heart.

A part of her wants to move towards the sound, feels the pull of something, perhaps as simple as the warmth of another human, and so she goes, three, four, five steps deeper into the trees–

But the warmth is moving again, away from her.

She's not worried. If it's who she is looking for, she will find him.

Of this – and maybe this alone – she is certain.

–the sweat quickly dripping from his nose in three, four, five black circles on the path's pavement. It had been months since it ended with Enzo, months spent happily with *Linus*, how ridiculously lucky was *that*, approaching the twelfth grade of a public high school in the sub-sub-suburbs? And they were good months, months full of laughter and tenderness.

So why did it still ache?

"You okay, son?" The old man on the home-made bicycle had caught up to him.

Adam popped out an earbud. "Just a broken heart."

"My advice?" The old man didn't stop, just kept slowly pedalling by. "Whiskey. And lots of it."

Adam laughed in a single syllable, shaking his head as he took off running again.

He was at the point – he checked his phone – just over thirty-five minutes in, where nothing hurt. His legs were in rhythm, his feet hitting their strike at the right cadence, his arms swinging their counterweight.

I feel strong, he thought, almost consciously. I feel *strong*. He ran a little faster.

Still, his parents loved him. They must. In their own way. But that way seemed to depend on an unspoken set of rules Adam was expected to know and abide by; and to be fair, he probably did know them. It was abidance that was a problem.

He had loved, though. And been loved himself. That he was sure of, even if it *was* Angela. Plus, she was the one who told him he was in love with Enzo (and, in fact, was the one who told Enzo that, too). He'd given his feelings for boys a name not long before then, had even already somehow lost his virginity (though that was another story), so it certainly wasn't just being oblivious, though Angela had proved strangely vehement about naming anything.

"Let's say I want to kiss Shelley Morgan," she'd said.

Adam had looked over from the throw pillows they were sharing on the floor of her family's TV room. "You do?"

"Well, kind of. I mean, who doesn't? She's part-vampire, part-baby marmot."

"And that does it for you?"

"It does it for most people who aren't you. Now, shut up, I'm making a point: I'd also be interested in kissing Kurt Miller."

"Ugh, you already have, though. And all that peach fuzz."

"Really? I find it endearing. But say I want to kiss

both Shelley and Kurt and I want to do this on the same day. What would that make me?"

"Hungry?"

"No, you're supposed to say 'bi' and I'm supposed to yell at you. Or you were supposed to say 'slut' and I'd *really* yell at you."

They waited a moment while a handsome-but-stupid-and-very-waxed frat jock got flayed by the hillbilly zombie in the movie they'd downloaded. One of the many things Adam and Angela bonded over was a shared hatred of drippy teen movies. Horror all the way.

"Sick," Angela said, eating a Dorito.

"But *wouldn't* that make you bi, though?"

"Oh, my God, *no*, you label fascist!"

"There it is."

"My point: why do you have to call yourself anything? Because, if you don't, freedom. Because, self-actualization. Because, fluidity and not calcifying into what that label will make you."

"How about, because having an identity can be just as powerful as actualizing my fluidity?"

"But are you *sure* you only like boys? Why not keep your options open?"

"Because my entire upbringing has told me there was only one way to be. That any other way is wrong. A deviation from their certainty."

"All the more reason to–"

"I'm not finished. When I realized how things were, when I said to myself that I am *not* this thing I've been told

43

I have to be, that I am *this other thing* instead, then Jesus, Ange, the label didn't feel like a prison, it felt like a whole new freaking map, one that was my own, and now I can take any journey I want to take and it's possible I might even find a home there. It's not a reduction. It's a *key*."

Angela ate another Dorito, thoughtfully. "Okay," she said. "I can see that."

"And if I felt anything like that for a girl, don't you think it would only ever be you?"

"Oh, fuck off, Disney Channel, you're way too tall for me." But she scooted across the Darlingtons' shag carpet and put her head on his shoulder. She stared at the screen for a minute while a topless blonde was beheaded. "I think I want to kiss Shelley more than Kurt, though."

"Whatever, I promise never to call you anything until you tell me to."

"And I promise not to care about your small-minded label because you insist it's liberating."

"Good." He kissed the top of her head.

"Now, when are you going to get into Enzo Garcia's pants already?"

"Enzo?" He'd been genuinely surprised. And then, suddenly, not. "Oh," he said. "Oh, yeah."

And that was how, not three weeks later, at Angela's sixteenth birthday party (she was four months older and surprisingly gracious about not lording it over him), the only other guests besides Adam were a pleasantly surprised Enzo and a slightly baffled but really quite sweet Shelley Morgan.

"Here's how it is," Angela said in a low voice to

Adam and Enzo after her parents had dropped them off at the bowling alley. "I'm going to spend this whole evening seeing how well worth getting to know better Shelley is, and you two need to leave us to it. Fortunately, Enzo, Adam is totally in love with you, so you'll have lots to talk about."

She'd left them to their stunned silence, Adam realizing too late that he should have been laughing it off immediately.

He hadn't. Enzo noticed. At the end of the night, they kissed in a shadow outside. Enzo tasted of pretzels and warm, his lips as soft as a sleepy puppy. Adam had almost been literally dazed, like he'd never been so thirsty.

Angela ended up kissing Shelley Morgan, too, but said that *she* had smelled of grape. "It was like kissing a Care Bear."

That had started Enzo and Adam, though. All seventeen months, one week, and three days of it.

Adam passed six miles where the path on the lakeside started a long curve back into the woods. His music still blasted in his ears, but it all somehow felt silent back here. The path was empty, the lake steadily disappearing behind thickening trees. His breath pulled one pattern over the slightly different one of his feet. He passed into some shadow and the sudden coolness made him realize how wet with sweat he was, his shirt soaked all the way down to the hem.

He checked his phone again. No wonder. The running app showed he was at top pace. One that, if he'd been able to keep it up over all these distances rather than so late into them, might have made him a competitive cross-country runner after all.

Maybe Angela's joke, if that's what it was, had been the problem with Enzo in the end. She was trying to be helpful, assuming Enzo was just as interested in Adam, but if he wasn't, she had effectively handed over all of Adam's power in one simple sentence.

"Do you really love me?" Enzo had asked, just before they kissed, a smile half disbelieving, half intrigued across that beautifully handsome face of his.

And why not? It was so much easier to be loved than to have to do any of the desperate work of loving.

A square slab of grey concrete abruptly ends the treeline. She almost falls into the empty air, as if a wall has been removed.

She stands, astonished.

I am here.

There are cuts on her feet from her walk through the forest. The ground was littered not only with the green detritus of a mature woodland but the garbage of humans. Broken glass, a rusted shopping cart, so very much plastic in a limitless array of colours, all of them ugly, and in one small clearing, a bed of used hypodermic needles that stabbed her feet as she walked over them, bite after bite, until she looked as if she'd been attacked by a porcupine.

Though she does not bleed. And the pain is so distant as to be in another room.

Ahead of her now, across the square of concrete, stands a closed-down convenience store, fading to dereliction.

I have thirst, she thinks.

"I have thirst," she says aloud.

"You won't find any help there, little lady," a voice answers.

A man. His clothes, his skin, his hair, all the colour of camouflaging dust, hiding him as he sits in the shadow of an elderly dumpster along the side of the building.

She tries to answer, tries to ask him what he means, but her mouth struggles and all she is able to say is, "I have thirst" again, frowning at the effort.

The man leans out of the shadows to get a better look at her. His face is a mask of beard and sun-damaged wrinkles, but the concern there is plain. "Are you coming down off something?" His voice changes, as if he is talking to himself. "Probably meth, yeah, probably meth, all those labs out there in the trees, but the face, the face, meth melts your face, and that face ain't melted, that face is the sun on water, man, the sun on water, the sun on the water." He speaks up again. "Do you need a doctor?"

The word "meth" has turned a queer screw in her belly, a cold one, a fearful one, and words again come up from inside, floating like a choke of feathers, I don't, I don't, I don't–

"I don't," she says.

"I look at her," the man says, "and I don't know if this is the truth she speaks, if these words are even the answer to my question, and the sun that hits my face is not, it is not, the same sun that hits her face, a sun cast through water, a sun dappled, moving, breathing."

He stands, then seems surprised to find himself standing.

His voice reaches out once more. "You have nothing to fear from me." He stretches back into the shadow and picks up a black can, already opened. "I can help you with your thirst, though to be honest, you probably shouldn't drink too much. Not in this heat. Not with the sun shining on you like that."

He steps towards her. "Here, my lady, I don't expect you to come to me. You can't expect her to do that. You'll have to go to her. You will. You must. But will she harm you?"

"I will not," she says, discovering it is true as she says it.

The man crosses the grey concrete, his gait stiff, painful, but steady. He stops slightly more than arm's length from her. He holds out the can, straining to reach her, as if he can come no closer.

She steps to him instead, taking the offering hand in both of hers, steadying it. He gasps, astonished at the physical contact. She can smell him now, a smudge of unwashed skin, poverty, extreme loneliness. She takes the can, still holding his hand, unrolling it, running a finger across its weathered palm.

"This hand," she says. "This hand killed me."

"Not this hand."

"A hand like it."

"All hands are alike. As alike as they are different."

She releases his palm, finds herself still holding the can, a remarkable odour of yeast pressing from it, almost alive.

She drinks. The taste is a railroad train, the boom of

a timpani, a lighthouse through fog. She laughs aloud, the foam running down her chin.

"God, I hated *this stuff*," she says, in a voice that is entirely hers and entirely someone else's. It shocks her into silence.

I have never drunk this before, she thinks.

I have drunk this before and hated it, she thinks.

"Both are true," she says.

"They always are," the man says.

"Tell me. How many of me do you see?"

"I'll see as many of you as you wish."

She wonders if he speaks true, if he will be able to answer the questions that hover here, just above and behind her, a flock of watchful birds, waiting for her to stumble. How is she here? Where is she going? What is this thorn in her heart and what does it bind there?

But no. He is troubled by his state, she can see that now. He is a damaged human, as so many of them are (them? she thinks), and he struggles through the best he can manage. She can't even feel disappointment, only pity.

"Thank you," *she says, handing him back the can with a deep seriousness.*

"She gives it back to you," *the man says.* "She turns the sun to you and she thanks you."

"I do."

"She thanks you."

The man watches as she crosses the square of concrete, wading out towards an unbusy road, an intent seriousness seeming to drive her, one that ignores the broken ground punishing her feet.

"She leaves," he says, drinking from the can.

He keeps the same unsurprised expression when the faun steps onto the square of concrete, hooves clopping like a prim donkey's. He is seven feet tall, furred to his haunches, horned of head, bare of chest, naked as a wild creature, his priapic goat smell clearing the man's nostrils as effectively as any menthol. He reaches for the man.

"It's touching your eyes," the man says. "It's a dream, this. It can only be. It offers you forgetfulness and the forgetfulness is sweet."

The faun leaves the man standing there, in a euphoria that will be the only thing he'll remember of this encounter. The faun hurries after her, glancing up at the now midmorning sun. The day is long, but it is not endless.

He has until dusk. He has only until dusk.

Adam crossed the seven-mile mark as he finished the little segment of lakeside path. One mile from home, unless he wanted to turn left and add another four. But all that was out that way was a closed 7-Eleven and probably half the meth labs in the county. He might have, regardless, and had done so on his very best running days (and his very worst), but today he had no time.

He turned right instead, running through the parking lot at the end of the trail, noticed his brother's truck there, his brother behind the wheel.

"Adam!" Marty shouted, loud enough to be heard over Adam's playlist.

"Not stopping!" he yelled back. He turned onto a back country road – shoulderless, of course, it was an ongoing miracle that he'd never been knocked into a ditch – and kept at full pace. Halfway down this road, he'd pass the western fence of Angela's farm. You couldn't see her house from there, but her horse and its companion goat might be grazing.

"Hey, bro," his bro said, pulling alongside in the truck, keeping pace, waiting for Adam to turn down his music. "I honked for you when you started on the lakeside. Guess you must not have heard me."

"Sure."

"Get in. I want to talk to you."

"No. And I thought you were helping Dad."

"Yeah, well." Marty's voice had a surprising hitch in it, enough to make Adam look over, but not enough to make him stop.

His golden brother. Hair so blond it was almost white, facial hair that faded to lighter blond rather than the usual ginger, a strapping set of shoulders, a smile that would normally have made him the world's most successful youth pastor, if – and this was his father's point about effectiveness – Marty hadn't been the most boring Sunday School teacher Adam had ever had. If the rumours were true, Marty had also matured into the most boring preacher in his entire seminary.

When you were that handsome, everyone assumed you could work an audience, so often that no one ever actually bothered showing you *how*. Physical beauty, of all the curses, was obviously the best you could get. It was still a curse, though.

"He wasn't happy with the suggestions I made for his sermon tomorrow," Marty said, puttering alongside Adam. "The words 'grade-school hokum' were used."

"Dad's from Oregon. Why does he talk like an Appalachian hick?"

"They call it 'folksiness' in seminary."

"I'm on the home stretch, Marty. I really need to concentrate–"

"Get in. I'll drive you."

"And again, no." He kept moving. Marty kept pace, watching out for traffic behind them. The road was deserted, which was why Adam used it.

Marty was starting his senior year in a couple of weeks, too, at a church college in rural Idaho, one that was training him to preach and to minister, with an eye to being taken on at The House Upon The Rock and maybe, one day, being the second-generation Thorn as head pastor. This was something Marty wanted very badly, despite what was slowly being confirmed as his complete unsuitability to do so.

"Listen, bro–"

Adam finally stopped. "I'm in the middle of something, Marty! I mean, seriously, have you gone blind or has seminary just made you so sure you're the important one that no one else's lives matter?"

"Whoa, where's all this coming from?"

"What do you *want*?" Adam was aware of Angela's horse and its companion goat behind him over the fence, coming closer, chewing their grass, interested in the gossip.

Marty didn't answer him at first, just sat there, his truck idling. "It'd be easier if you got in–"

"Marty–"

"I'm going to be a father."

Adam blinked. So did the horse and the companion

55

goat. The sentence was so incongruous that at first Adam misunderstood. "You're becoming Catholic?"

Marty looked startled, then rolled his eyes. "Not that kind of father."

Adam stepped closer to the open passenger side window of the truck. "You mean...?"

"Yeah."

"Are you shitting me?"

Marty closed his eyes. "I'd really appreciate it if you wouldn't swear–"

"You got Katya *pregnant*?"

Katya was Marty's long-time girlfriend. Beautiful, Belarusian, teensy bit racist about the Jews, if we're being honest. She – through some impossibly convoluted chain of patronage and government sponsorship – had somehow ended up studying engineering at the same rural Christian college as Marty. As likely the two prettiest people on campus, possibly in all of Idaho, their coupling had an inevitability to it. When Katya visited, she brought her own scales to weigh her portions of food. Adam's parents were terrified of her.

Adam saw his brother swallow. "Not Katya," Marty said.

"Not..." Adam put his hands on the window ledge. "Oh, Marty. What have you done?"

Marty took out his phone, swiped a few times and brought up a picture. A very pretty (of course) black girl looked off-screen, laughing, holding a blue plastic disposable cup, the kind you got at parties (not get-togethers).

She was Marty's age and wearing a sweatshirt of the church college. Marty had never mentioned her before in his life.

"Her name's Felice," he said, smiling to himself. "It means happy."

"Well," Adam deadpanned, "that makes everything okay then. What's her sign?"

Marty's blond eyebrows started a conversation with themselves. "Leo? I think? Why on earth–"

"Marty! How the hell could you get her pregnant? Are you a complete idiot about contraception? Is *she*?"

"The school frowns on it," Marty said, frowning on it.

"More than pregnancy?"

"We never meant to go that far–"

"Wait a minute." Adam was quickly losing his running heart rate. His muscle tissue would already be swelling for post-run healing. He was basically going to cool off into a golem if he didn't start running again very soon. "Why are you telling *me*? Why did you track me down on a *run* to–" His eyes narrowed. "You haven't told Mom and Dad."

Marty at least had the grace to look sheepish. "I had to tell somebody."

Adam exhaled. "She's going to have it, of course."

"Of course! Abortion is out of the–"

"For her or for you?"

"For both of us!"

"Sometimes it's the wisest course of action, bro."

57

Marty shook his head, disappointed. "Dad's right about you. You got lost on your journey somewhere."

"That's what everyone says who never bothered to go on a journey in the first place. And–" he halted his brother's apology, which he could already see coming– "we can take comfort in the fact that Dad was *completely* wrong about *you*."

They were quiet for a minute, the road still deserted, only the idling of the truck engine cutting across the dew-filled morning. The horse and the goat still stood and chewed, blamelessly curious. Adam ran his hand through his sweat-slicked hair.

"Are you going to marry her?"

Marty nodded. "She only found out yesterday and called me." He grinned. "I proposed immediately."

"Over the phone?"

"She's talking to her folks in Denver right now. I'm telling Mom and Dad this weekend. If we both survive, we're going to get married as soon as senior year starts. The university has special housing for married undergrads."

"Where? 1952?"

Marty laughed, gently. He always laughed gently.

"What do you want from me?" Adam asked. "Congratulations? You got 'em. Based on the thirty seconds I've known about her existence and the one photo you've shown me, I'm thrilled for the both of you."

"I love her. I mean, I really love her. And she says she loves me the same."

"What happened to Katya?"

"Katya was kinda mean."

"No kidding."

Marty looked sheepish again. "I was going to tell Mom and Dad tonight while you're at your get-together. I don't suppose…"

"Don't suppose what?"

"Don't suppose you've got anything big *you* want to tell them first?"

"What?"

"I figure if it's both of us, then the heat gets split in two. Less for each."

"Anything big to tell them like what?" Adam held his brother's stare, daring Marty to say it out loud. Marty didn't, so Adam went on. "No matter how mad they're going to be at you for this – and they will be – at the end of it, they get a grandchild. You weather the storm, there's a happy ending for you." He couldn't stop himself from adding, "Like there always is."

"Not always," Marty said.

"More often than me."

Marty shook his head again. "You're still just a kid. You wouldn't even know what it is to fall in love yet. You will, though, one day. I hope."

"You're twenty-two, Marty. What do you think *you* know about love?"

"Bro–"

"If Felice isn't the first girl you've slept with, then she's the second, right?"

"I don't see what that has to do–"

59

"Well, *one*, my sex life is already more vibrant than yours–"

"I don't want to hear about that–"

"And two, I know what it is to be in love, Marty."

"No, you don't. Teenage love isn't love. Especially if it's..." He stopped.

"Especially if it's what?" Adam leaned into the truck, raised his voice. "Especially if it's *what*?"

Marty looked genuinely distressed. "You think they don't know? You think they don't talk to me about you all the time?"

"They never talk to *me* about me, so I just imagined they did their best not to think about it at all."

"Look, I'm not..." Marty threw his hands in the air, failed to grab the word he wanted, rested them again on the steering wheel. "I love you, bro, but you have to know that this life you've chosen–"

"Tread carefully, Marty. I mean it. The world has completely changed around you while you weren't looking."

Marty looked Adam square in the eye. "It's not real love. Everybody's convinced themselves that it is, but it isn't. And it never will be."

Adam was so angry he felt winded, his airways struggling to get enough oxygen against the upswell of rage and hurt rising from his stomach. He wanted a line, a well-worded sentence he could hurl at Marty and wipe that maddening pity off his face, one that would incidentally destroy the truck somehow while annihilating his brother's empty-headed arrogance, one that would win this stupid, soul-sucking argument once and for all.

But all he got out was "*Ass*hole."

He took off running again, turning his music back up. The horse and the companion goat watched him go.

He *was* stiff, had cooled off painfully, and it felt like he was running in leg splints, but he didn't care. He ran anyway, leaving the truck behind.

I love you but…

It was always, *always*, "I love you but…"

He ran faster. And faster. And faster again.

This anger, he thought. This tedious, endless anger. Was that all there was ever going to be? Would it just twist him and twist him, obliterating everything else so he lost the ability to know when he *should* be angry because that was all there ever was?

He pushed, his strides growing longer, his hands opening and swinging higher into the sprint.

I don't want this, he thought. I don't want to be this person. I don't want to always fight.

I want to love.

I want to love.

I want to love Enzo.

His legs were at their physical limit. They felt disconnected from him, almost their own creatures, filled with a wobbly sting, like an injury in cold weather. If he stopped to think, he would lose his balance. Running was the only thing that kept him upright.

I want to love Linus, he thought.

I want to *want* to love Linus.

He approached his house from the opposite direction he'd driven away earlier this morning, down a small gully, his speed peaking, the fire hydrant as his finish line, the fire hydrant, the fire hydrant–

He passed it and let up, slowing to walk in a circle. His heart was pumping so hard he could see it pulse in his wrists, his chest gulping air like a goldfish flipped from its bowl.

The music still blasted in his earbuds. He saw his mom looking at him from under the brim of her very corny gardening hat. She had a degree in linguistics, was only forty-three years old, but for some reason insisted on dressing like a grandmother from a commercial for fancy cookies. Folksiness, he supposed. Though she'd have the grandmother thing sooner than she thought.

He continued his circle, huffing air, letting the pounding in his temples and ears recede. He'd twice pushed himself hard enough to vomit, and though it was awful, there felt something heroic in it, too, something powerful about going beyond what you could safely do, into oblivion, to the point where you could erase yourself, *be* erased.

For that reason, he didn't know now if his hands were shaking because of the run or because he was still raging.

He stopped, bending at the waist, trying to breathe through his nose. Without looking up, he turned off his music because his mom was clearly talking to him now. "What's that?"

"I said–" she ruthlessly cropped an uncooperative chrysanthemum– "I don't know why you always need to make such a big production out of it. It's just a run."

"What?"

She made a series of honking sounds so ugly, it took him a second to realize she was making fun of his breathing. "It's just a jog around town," she said. "It's not like you finished a marathon."

Adam swallowed once. "Marty got a girl pregnant."

She didn't even consider believing him. "Oh, drama, drama, drama. One day, you'll grow up, baby boy, and we'll all–"

"He's telling you and Dad this weekend. They're going to get married and live in housing the school provides for families."

She opened her mouth to respond, then closed it, then opened it again. "I don't like this kind of story, Adam. You think it's very amusing, but in the end, it's just a lie. And about your brother."

"Speak of the devil," Adam said, "and in he drives." For indeed, with timing so perfect he could have laughed, there was Marty's truck, cresting the gully behind him.

His mom was severe now. "This isn't funny, Adam."

"No. I don't suppose it is. I don't know where he's going to get the money to raise a baby *and* pay for his last year of school. Not with how strapped we are for cash right now."

They watched Marty pull to a stop. He looked out at their faces, trying to figure out how much trouble he was in. It was probably this that made it start to sink in for his mother.

"Katya?" she almost whispered.

"Nope," Adam said, turning his music back on and heading inside before all the shouting started.

He went straight to the shower, but within moments, he could hear them, even under the pouring water. His mother, mainly, wailing – there was really no other word for it – though possibly only because here was an opportunity to have a good wail rather than that she was genuinely that upset.

Marty came and pounded on the door of the bathroom. "Why?" he shouted through it. "Why, bro?"

Adam just laced his hands behind his neck and stuck his head under the torrent.

Why indeed?

His chest still burned, so much he couldn't tell where the anger stopped and the wound began. Because there was always a wound, it seemed, kept freshly opened by a family who also kept saying they loved him.

This was a day for crying, he knew that already, with Enzo leaving at the end of it. But not now. No. He wouldn't.

They sure did know where to shoot the arrow, though.

Because what if they were right? What if there *was* something wrong with him? What if, on some level, way down deep inside, right down to the very simplest, purified form of who he was, what if he *was* corrupted? What if there was some tiny, tiny fault in the first building blocks of who he was, and everything since that first moment of life was just papering over an essential crack?

And he was just a carapace built on a facade built on scaffolding and there was no real core to him, no real central worth? At all?

Can I love? he thought. *Can* I?

Can I *be* loved?

He finished the shower, dried himself, and – making sure Marty had left – snuck down the hall to his bedroom. He changed into his uniform for the Evil International Mega-Conglomerate – polyester, of course, but with some actual tailoring; the Evil International Mega-Conglomerate didn't want to make its customers uncomfortable by having them think they were being assisted by the *poor* – and picked up his keys, an outfit to change into at Linus's, and his phone.

He hesitated, then messaged, *Sorry for telling them, bro. But you need to say sorry, too.*

He sent it and tapped another name. *Marty got a girl pregnant,* he messaged. *Not even kidding.*

WHAT?!?! Angela messaged back. *Did he even READ Judy Blume?*

Things are kinda hairy over here. My mom is wailing.

You're so lucky. My parents never get upset about anything.

He smiled to himself, but only because he knew he was supposed to, that this was what he'd been asking for. He didn't feel it, though.

He waited and listened, trying to guess the right moment to slip out of the house without anybody seeing him.

3

EVIL INTERNATIONAL MEGA-CONGLOMERATE

The simple fact of it was that the Thorns were poorer than they looked. The house – chrysanthemums included – was owned by the church for tax reasons, and the Thorns, as the job's best perk, paid no rent on it. But nor did they own it, so they couldn't borrow against it to pay for things like Marty's and, presumably, Adam's upcoming tuition. Plus, the salary from The House Upon The Rock took into account the home as a benefit and was surprisingly not very much at all.

The situation was apparently different at The Ark of Life, Frome's largest evangelical church. It wasn't a rival to The House Upon The Rock – for how could churches be rivals, perish the thought, we're all doing God's Work – but Big Brian Thorn had competitiveness down to his bones. His years at The House Upon The Rock had been one long, unsuccessful plan to topple The Ark in both attendance and holiness in the God's Work team standings.

But it was still Ark Pastor Terry "The Hair" LaGrande and his wife Holly-June who had four congregations of a thousand-plus each stretching over even Saturday night. It was Terry and Holly-June whose sermons on the Prosperity Gospel didn't sound hollow because they drove a gold Mercedes. It was Terry and Holly-June who had three perfect brunette daughters, the eldest of whom had signed a recording contract with a contemporary Christian music label and was just about to release her first song, "Single Ladies (For Jesus)".

The Thorns did their best to have their externals match the LaGrandes. The internals – what with Adam's mom being laid off last year as a linguistic analyst for the Defense Department in Seattle – were held together pay cheque by precarious pay cheque. Adam worked all the hours possible just to keep himself in fresh clothes and gas to put into the twenty-year-old Honda he'd found on craigslist for four hundred dollars.

Which meant shifts in the massive stockroom of the Evil International Mega-Conglomerate under Wade Gillings, who still managed a stockroom, however massive, at thirty-eight, whose slacks were of alarming tightness, and who was way, way too handsy.

"Thorn!" he yelled as Adam passed the closet that served as Wade's insulting little office. A hand came out of the doorway to slap Adam's left butt cheek.

Adam closed his eyes. "We've had this discussion, Wade. I *will* go to human resources."

Wade, his moustache and feathered hair both several

decades out of sync with anything modern, made a sad puppy-dog face and whimpered, faux tearfully, "I'm Adam Thorn and my pussy hurts."

"Jesus, Wade–"

"You're late."

"No, I'm not."

"Almost. I could write you up for that."

"I'll only be late if you hold me here and stop me from clocking in."

Wade leered. "You want me to hold you, is that what you're saying?"

Adam turned to the pad on the wall installed with the time-keeping app, realizing too late he was keeping his back to Wade, who slapped Adam's *right* butt cheek, saying, "Get to work. Karen and Renee are in housewares."

Adam sighed and clocked in. His phone buzzed as he made his way to the houseware section of the vast warehouse at the back of the main store.

I'm sensing some lack of okayness about the ruckus at home, Angela had just messaged. *Am I high?*

No, he messaged back. *Just the usual.*

The usual hasn't historically been good. We'll make it better tonight tho.

Everything okay? What do we need to talk about?

All fine, worry hamster. Wade feel you up yet? Because, inappropriate.

Adam had known Angela since the third grade, but they hadn't become friends until their fifth-grade class took an overnight field trip to an observatory. It was Washington in October, so of course it was overcast, but the canny observatory owners had a planetarium as backup. Thirty ten-year-olds lay down their sleeping bags, heavily chaperoned by parents including Marieke Darlington, Angela's mom. They watched the universe unspool above them. But that only took fourteen minutes, so the observatory just ran it again. After the fourth run-through, mutiny fomented and an observatory worker ran a "laser show" that hadn't been on public view since the early eighties. Thirty drowsy ten-year-olds drifted off to the light-filled lullaby of *Dark Side of the Moon*.

Adam's dad texted the next morning to say he'd be an hour late picking him up because Mrs Navarre had requested a faith healing for her rheumatoid arthritis. "Is that a real reason?" Angela's mother had asked, but she offered him a ride home anyway. Adam and Angela sat quietly in the back seat as Mrs Darlington, a good ten years older than Adam's own mother, did most of the talking via the rear-view mirror.

"Did you have a good time?" she asked. "I mean, I know you didn't see any proper space stuff, but the planetarium show was nice, maybe not the last three times, and the laser show, my goodness, that took me back. I remember sneaking into one as a teenager in Holland with my sister and the pot smoke was so heavy, the lasers were almost 3-D. That's when your aunty Famke met your uncle Dirk, Angela, and might even be the night she got pregnant with your cousin Lucas."

"*Mom,*" Angela said, putting her face in her hands.

"What?" She glanced at Adam in the mirror. "I'm sorry, Adam, I didn't mean to embarrass you."

"You didn't embarrass me," Adam said. Quite the contrary, Mrs Darlington talked like no other mother he'd ever met. He wanted her to keep doing it at length.

"My parents believed," she continued, "that baby talk and avoiding topics was almost child abuse. That you'd end up raising swaddled little morons to send out into the world to be eaten alive. I preferred it when adults expected me to reach up to them rather than always leaning down to me. Do you see what I mean?"

"I do, actually," Adam said, which was how he spoke, even at ten. He saw Angela give him an astonished side-eye from underneath her hands. "I think my mom and dad would *still* rather not reach up."

Mrs Darlington laughed out loud at exactly the same moment a truck ran a stop sign and hit Mrs Darlington's car just behind Angela, spinning it across the intersection and over an embankment, down which it rolled sideways a complete circle and a half, coming to rest on its roof in what was luckily a very shallow creek.

Mrs Darlington was badly injured: a broken arm and hip surgery kept her out of farmwork for nearly a year. But in the back seat, tiny Angela and prepubescent Adam had been small enough to be shaken in their seat belts as the car tumbled but without having been struck by anything worse than a loose textbook that knocked out one of Angela's side teeth and blackened Adam's eye.

Adam remembered the seconds after they came to a stop, before Mrs Darlington regained consciousness and tried not to scare the children by moaning too loudly, when he and Angela were side by side, hanging upside down, still buckled in, blinking in shock. She had looked over to him in the sudden violent silence and reached out for his dangling hand.

She asked him, very seriously, "Is there homework?"

"I did mine after breakfast," he said back, "when Jennifer Pulowski was having that meltdown about her parents' divorce."

"Oh, yeah," Angela said, still stunned. "Me, too." That's when she turned back to the front seat and said, her voice breaking, "Momma?"

Adam and Angela had been firm friends ever since. They'd nearly died together, after all, which seemed a solid basis. He kind of loved the Darlingtons. He definitely loved Angela. If you could choose your family, he'd definitely choose them. And maybe he already had. He looked at his phone again and wondered about her as he found Karen and Renee in housewares.

"All I know is," Karen said, scanning the label for some non-stick frying pans, "my dad said that if I ever got near a meth lab, he'd send me to live with my grandmother in Alaska. *Alaska*. There are supposed to be twenty-three of these."

"*Please*," Renee said, nodding at Adam as she saw him approaching. "Like black people ever do meth. Six, twelve, eighteen, there's twenty-two."

"The black people in Alaska probably do," Karen said, typing in the stock loss. "The ones who aren't my grandmother."

"Both of them?" Renee said. "Hey, Adam. Why is this a three-person job?"

"I shelve and unshelve," he said. "Wade wants housewares and guns done by this afternoon."

"Wade wants to look at your ass in that uniform, is what he wants," Karen said, scanning a slightly larger non-stick frying pan. "This says we're supposed to have 27.2. How can you have point two of a frying pan?"

"How can you *scan* point two of a frying pan?" Renee said.

Adam took the scanning wand, whacked it hard with his hand, and handed it back. Karen scanned again. "Twenty-seven." She looked up, deadpan. "Thank you for whacking my wand, Adam."

"Any time." He started unshelving the next section of housewares, which was every variety of saucepan.

Karen and Renee were cousins, in Adam's year at school, inseparable convention-going geeks, and worked every shift together. One time they came in pre-con cosplay as two-fifths of a black Jem and the Holograms under their uniforms. Wade didn't even notice.

"You guys talking about the murder?" Adam asked.

"Yeah," Karen said, the smaller of the two. "Renee knew Katherine van Leuwen in Girl Scouts."

"A million years ago, when she was still Katie," Renee said, taller but quieter around anyone else besides Karen.

She had the beginnings of insulin injection scars on her torso. She'd shown him once. "She was nice. Kinda lost, though. Even then."

"Little girls aren't naturally lost," Karen said, frowning as she scanned saucepans. "Someone makes them that way."

"You sound like Angela," Adam said, reshelving frying pans.

"More people should sound like Angela."

"I don't disagree."

"I get nightmares about being strangled," Renee said. "You know I can't even wear scarves."

"She really can't," Karen said. "Fire would be worse, though. Fire would be way worse."

"Fire's faster. You know for a long time you can't breathe before you get strangled."

They worked in silence for a minute while they all considered this. Adam reshelved the counted saucepans and unshelved the uncounted bundles of cutlery, which weighed a ton.

"Do black people really not do meth?" he asked.

"Nope," Karen said. "That's just stupid crackers out in the woods."

She stands in the backyard of a cabin. It's quiet, closed in by trees on three sides, a gravel drive and a second cabin on the fourth. The cabins are long unused; the grass reaches her knees.

But there is yellow police tape around this one.

She starts a slow walk, pressing down the grass until she comes across newer tracks near the front, left by many feet, into and out of the small front door.

"I know this place," she says, to no one, to the faun, who she cannot see but who watches from the edge of the trees.

This is the lake cabin, she thinks, one of the cheap ones, across a forlorn road and away from the lake shore. One that used to be serviced by the convenience store she's just come from. One that was closed around the same time the convenience store was.

But one that was still used, illegally.

"How do I know these things?" she says, frowning to herself.

• • •

The faun wishes to tell her, tell her that she is caught, his Queen, snagged and bound by a frightened soul. He needs to tell her that she is in danger of becoming lost forever, but he cannot. He can only look at the sun, less than an hour from its midday peak. The faun is worried. The faun is very worried.

She crosses the grass to the front of the cabin. Hesitating only for a second, she steps up, onto the porch, pulling aside the yellow tape. The front door is open, and she pauses there.

She can smell violence. Terrible things have happened here. Not once, but many times, over many years. The despair of humans. Their fear. The violence they do themselves.

"The violence we do ourselves," she whispers.

An anger rises. She pushes the door, sudden, fast, so hard it falls off its hinges. She storms in, her bare feet raising burn marks on the floor, whiffs of smoke vanishing as she steps. "You are here! You are here! You would do this to me?"

She stops in the middle of the room. She is alone, wonders why she thought she wasn't.

But it was the past, of course.

"I know this place," she says once more.

She kneels and touches a bare spot on the knotty

wooden floor, cleared among the detritus of junkies: food wrappers, used toilet paper, syringes, and a stench that's almost a presence in itself.

"It was here." She turns suddenly to the faun, now in the doorway himself. "Wasn't it?"

He starts for a moment. "Yes," he says, "it was, my lady, can you—"

But she does not see him. She is not speaking to him.

"It was here," she says again.

He watches as she places her palm flat against the floor-boards. Smoke rises from where she burns it.

"This is where I died."

"You going to Enzo's thing tonight?" Renee asked him, shyly.

Karen and Renee didn't officially know about Adam and Enzo, no one *officially* did, maybe not even Adam and Enzo, but they knew it in the unofficial way everyone who had been even slightly observant knew (and not wilfully blind like certain parents he could name). No one under twenty seemed to care, but they weren't the ones who ruled his life at home.

"Yeah," Adam answered. "You guys?"

"Yep," Karen said. "I'm not a big fan of the lake, though. Too cold."

"No one's going to swim." Renee looked mildly terrified. "Are they?"

Adam said he didn't know. "Angela and I are bringing pizzas from her work, though."

"Why?" Karen asked, scanning end tables, which was easy, as there were only ever one or two. Renee and Adam didn't have to do anything, so everyone was taking their time.

"Why?" Adam repeated. "Why not?"

"His mom's a doctor. It's not like they can't get their own son's pizza."

"They're paying for it," Adam said, though now that he thought about it, he couldn't recall any mechanism being discussed as to how that would actually happen. *Had* he heard them say they'd pay? "I volunteered," he said, pondering it.

"That was good of you," Karen said, not looking at him.

"Karen," Renee warned, gently.

"What?" Karen said. "If he wants to keep doing stuff for someone and getting nothing back, that's totally not my business, is it?"

"I don't–" Adam started. "He doesn't–" He unnecessarily shelved an end table. "Anyway, he's leaving town so there's no point talking about it. And who says there's anything to talk about?"

"Ain't no shame in a broken heart," Karen sang under her breath. Adam pretended not to hear.

Why *was* he bringing all the pizza? And maybe paying for it. (No. No, the Garcias were nice people. Busy but nice.) He was Enzo's friend, wasn't he? Isn't that what friends did? Friends with an aching chasm of pain between them that only one of them seemed able to see?

"You don't take any of this seriously, do you?" Enzo had said on their last night together before they became "friends". It was some months after Enzo had told Adam he loved him for the last time. And two seconds after Adam said it for what he didn't know was *his* last time.

"We're just messing around," Enzo said, not meeting Adam's eyes. "That's all."

At first he thought Enzo was kidding, *had* to be kidding. What had sixteen months been if not serious? What, if not love? "Just teenage experimental shit," Enzo said now. That's what.

It was a moment where Adam could have saved ... what? His self-respect at least. An ending that was true. But he'd seen the panic on Enzo's face, a face he knew *so* well, a mouth he'd kissed, eyes he'd seen laugh and cry. Enzo was terrified and that threw Adam, just enough.

"Yeah." He'd forced a laugh. "Just messing around." He forced another laugh. "All that I love you stuff, ha, ha, ha."

"I mean," Enzo said, "I'm not against doing it now and then, but it's just friends helping each other out before we get girlfriends, yeah?"

"I don't want a girlfriend," Adam had at least managed to say.

"Yeah, well, I do," Enzo said, not looking at him again.

Because if Adam was honest, was this actually so much of a surprise? If he really gathered all the things Enzo had said to him, had he really ever said "I love you" or had he only ever said "I love you, too"?

He was different than Adam, is what Adam always

told himself. Adam used words. Enzo used affection, didn't he? And he *had* been affectionate. If he hadn't said the words out loud much, he'd said them over and over again with a touch, with a kiss, with sex that was hardly just going in one direction.

"Why do we have to label it?" Enzo had asked, all along, it was true. "Why can't we just *be*?"

And Adam had said, "Okay." He'd said, "Okay." He hadn't even tried the it's-not-a-label-it's-a-map thing he'd sold to Angela. Why not? Why hadn't he? Why the hell did he just take whatever Enzo offered? Without argument or demand. Without even apparent self-respect.

Because he loved Enzo. Maybe there didn't have to be any other reasons. Maybe love made you stupid.

Maybe loneliness did.

Because: the day Adam got his driver's licence. That day.

It was two months after Adam turned sixteen, six months in with Enzo. Adam assumed he'd failed his test after bumping a kerb while parallel parking, but the examiner – a rumpled man who seemed genuinely on the edge of tears, so perhaps was nursing some fresh private grief – hadn't seemed to notice or much care about anything. He passed Adam without even looking up from his clipboard.

Adam had taken Enzo out in his mom's car – after promising not to go near any freeway and to call every hour to reassure her that he hadn't wrecked anything and was, incidentally, not dead. They had ignored the state law

84

that said new licensees could only drive their siblings for the first six months. "We look like brothers anyway," Enzo said. They didn't.

They'd gone to Denny's, celebrating the good news with deep-fried mozzarella sticks and Moons Over My Hammy.

"Let's go to the lake," Enzo had said, when they finished.

"We go to the lake all the time," Adam said.

"Not on our own. Not to the far side."

"There's nothing on the far side."

At which Enzo smiled.

The far side of the lake was officially state park. Unofficially, mostly due to budget cuts, it was a place where less-than-legal fields of pot were grown, and there were lurid and preposterous rumours of a forest cult and sightings of half-naked men in the furs of who knew what animals.

"It's daylight," Enzo said. "We'll be fine."

"Not daylight for much longer." Adam hated that the thought of driving out there made him nervous, but it did. If not the actual danger, then for what would happen if his parents found out. Though that was true of a lot of things these days.

"I know," Enzo said. "That's what I want to show you."

So they'd gone, Enzo directing him along lakeside roads that looked a lot less dangerous than legend made them out to be, though they did drive past the cabin where Katherine van Leuwen would eventually be murdered, so perhaps legend was on to something.

"Where are we going?" Adam asked.

"A secret place."

"Which you know about how?"

"I don't for sure. I found it online." He glanced over at Adam. "When I was thinking about what to get you."

"You were thinking about me?" Adam's chest lightened at even the thought. He also got half a hard-on and had to fight to keep from giggling.

Ridiculous.

"Turn here," Enzo said, "and it should be…"

"Whoa," Adam said, pulling to a stop in a small parking lot that looked all but forgotten. Ahead of them, a quirk in the trees made a perfect frame for Mount Rainier, bold as a tomcat, turning an unseemly, intimate pink as it stared across at the sunset.

"Best secret view around here," Enzo said. "Apparently."

"Cool," Adam said, a wholly inadequate word for the unexpected beauty of it, almost as if the mountain – a source of justifiable vanity for everyone who lived here – had been gathered for a private view, just for the eyes of Adam. Given to him by Enzo.

That was love, wasn't it? Enzo had taken time to think of him, taken time to do something as a gift to celebrate the new licence, thought ahead to the time he'd spend with Adam.

"I love you," Adam said, eyes firmly on the mountain.

"I know," Enzo replied, not unkindly, not *unlovingly*, just stating a simple fact.

"My mom and dad," Adam said, swallowing a knot away. "I don't know what I'd do without you, Enzo."

"I know that, too." And he'd put a hand on Adam's arm, then up to his head, bringing him over for a kiss, then another, and if he said, "There's something else this parking lot is famous for", and if Enzo had also thought ahead to bring condoms and if they then did the famous thing right there in the front seat of Adam's mother's Kia, if all that was true, it *remained* true that Enzo had thought about the view of the mountain, had saved it for Adam, had said to Adam when they were undressed, "You are *so* beautiful", with the face of someone looking past the physical.

How could that not be love?

"I love you," Adam said again, pale and naked under Enzo's darker, amusingly hairier body.

"And oh how I love you, too, Adam Thorn," Enzo said, kissing Adam's eyelids, deep in his rhythm.

Oh how I love you, too. Adam held on to that embarrassingly long in the months that followed, the months that somehow led to "We're just messing around."

Because evidently that's all Enzo had talked himself into thinking they were doing.

Adam hadn't even told Angela exactly how it had ended, and he told her *everything*. He'd hinted instead that it was sixty–forty mutual when it was really one hundred to zero. Even then, Angela had been ready to burn the earth Enzo walked on.

"I'll kill him," she said.

"It's okay."

"You are clearly *not* okay."

"It's just ... disappointment, that's all. We'll still be friends. It's cool."

"I don't know why you're lying to me." She took his hand and held it, just like that day they'd turned over in the car. "But maybe that's what you have to do to stay alive right now, so that's okay. If you ever fall, I'm here to catch you. Or not, actually, you're a giant, but I'm here to at least watch you fall and then get bandages."

He couldn't tell her that if he spoke the truth aloud, if he revealed everything he'd invested in Enzo, all that hope and possibility, all the life that was his own and no one else's, if he even *cried*, that would really mean it was over. Enzo went away, maybe he was scared, maybe he was screwed up a little in the head over the seriousness of it, or maybe he was going through some other stuff; his parents were pretty regular Catholics after all.

He would come back. He might come back. And so that bridge could never burn.

That last night had been more than ten months ago. Angela had tolerated him remaining friendly with Enzo, but it gradually became less of an issue for all of them, not just because of time passing – though mostly because of time passing – but also because of Linus. Who Adam loved. Who he wanted to love. Who maybe it was too early to love, but still, they said it. The bridge to Enzo hadn't burned, but it had been closed for use and, for some decent stretches of time, not thought of much at all.

Except when it was. Except when the bridge needed pizza before it moved to Atlanta.

Is this what Marty meant? When he said it wasn't real love? Did all this prove him wrong? Or did it prove him right?

Adam felt his eyes fill, was surprised, but maybe not. That wound in his chest, that thorn that seemed stuck there, however much it was real love or it wasn't (it was), none of that stopped it from hurting when Enzo left.

"He broke my heart," Adam said, out loud, to Karen and Renee.

They stared at him in the hanging dust of the stockroom. It was the most direct he'd ever been, the most he'd ever said to them.

"We know," Renee said.

"Stupid," Adam whispered to himself, thumbing away the tears that perched in his eyes.

"But he's leaving," Karen said. "Which is probably good and bad."

"Probably," Adam said.

"And you've got Linus Bertulis," Renee said, "don't you?"

"We like Linus," Karen said. "He's a nerd."

"A cute nerd," Renee said.

"Maybe that's enough of my private life for today–"

"I would sure as shit hope so," Wade said, coming around the corner. "If it's a bad idea for me to let friends work together, let me know and I can reduce everyone's hours."

Karen and Renee got right back to work, scanning the last of the end tables. Adam went to help them, but Wade grabbed his elbow. "After you get through the guns, I need to see you in my office."

Adam held the grasped arm away from himself like it was about to get a vaccination. "I'm off at one, Wade. I've got things to do."

"Then you'd better finish the guns pretty darn fast, don't you think?" He play-hit Adam in the stomach a little too hard and left them there.

"Asshole," Karen said under her breath.

"Has he talked to *you* guys in his office?" Adam asked.

They shook their heads. Karen holstered the stock-taking scanner. "Let's do guns now, get it over with. Nobody gives a damn if unscented candle stock is missing anyway."

"Man," Renee said, "I hate guns."

She sees her death, feels the hands around her neck, feels the bruises reappear on her grey skin. She presses her palm into the spot where it happened. The smoke rises from between her splayed fingers and her throat closes again, remembering the breath that would not come, the unbearable need to swallow that would not be satisfied. The fear was an increasing thing, rising in her gullet – though where would it go with her throat closed off?

She can remember no argument, no hostility even, from, from, from, from–

"Tony," she says, aloud, as the first flames lick up from her fingertips.

He was a mess, all meth heads were a mess, but he had mostly been a benign one. She was afraid of the boy-friend before Tony – Victor, all neck and rage – *but not Tony, never Tony.*

You took my stash, *Tony said, hands around her neck.*

"I didn't," she says now, the fire spreading out from her in a circle along the dried wood. "I didn't."

They had shot up together. He had given her the drugs himself. She hadn't gone near–

You took my stash, *Tony said again, and that was when the fear cut through the thousand beats per minute of the meth.*

"I am going to die," she says.

You did, you took it.

"I didn't."

You did.

She had. She wanted to tell him, now, at last. She had put it in her pocket when he closed his eyes as the meth first hit, but she wanted to tell him she was going to share it, that it was only because he lost it the last time, that it was for safe keeping–

"And I believe these things to be true as I think them," she says. *She wonders if they were.*

Tony moved his thumbs to the base of her throat for a clearer grip, a harder one that made her gag, made her vomit into the small glimpses of airway she had when Tony moved. There was no breath now. Not a chance of it.

She could distantly see Tony crying.

I loved you, *he wept, as he killed her.* I loved you.

Did you? *she had thought as the oxygen left her brain, as a kind of smouldering hole sunk through her consciousness, taking everything down with it.*

All the goatmen, *Tony said, bafflingly.* Don't think

I don't see them. Out there by the lake. And it's gone when you look.

The fire spreads to the drug detritus littering the floor. It catches quickly, filling the room with smoke, but she does not notice.

She sees the vision of Tony leaning up from her body, his dumb rage slipping from him slowly, even with the meth.

Kate? *he says.* Katie?

She watches him fumble backwards, his movements slow, clumsy, a kind of idiot shock taking over his features. Shit, *he says.* Oh, shit.

She watches as he scrambles for his needle, takes another hit of meth, waits for it, checks her again.

She is still dead.

"But oh," she says now. "Oh, oh, oh. That's it, is it not? Oh, oh, oh."

She watches Tony stand, watches him weep as he puts his hands under her arms, hefting her weight – so light, so frightfully light – over his shoulder. He weeps as he searches the cabin and finds one, two scavenged bricks to stuff into the pockets of her dress. He weeps as he steps through the flames that have become an inferno in the cabin and out the front door, carrying her body to the water.

"No," she says now. "No."

One wall of the cabin suddenly falls away, then a second, taking the roof with it. She watches as the third and fourth similarly fall, leaving her now on a burning foundation, at the centre of a fire she cannot feel

93

and that does not touch the rags of the clothes she still wears.

She looks up at nothing. "I was not yet dead. I was alive when he put me in the lake."

"Yes, my Queen," says the faun, unheard, winded from the controlled destruction of the cabin. "And that is why you are in such danger."

They were nearly finished with the guns. The actual pieces themselves were, of course, chained, locked, kept "safe", with the ammunition stored in another part of the vast warehouse. Still, anyone with the will and half an hour could break in here and easily find enough for a medium-sized massacre.

Adam and Renee handled the double-key locks, while Karen leaned in the cages with the scanning wand, trying to get through them as fast as possible. For once, they had to be meticulous. If anything was missing, it was a police matter. Then again, it would also be a police matter if they found out three minors were doing this stock-taking, so it was all a bit of a grey area, really.

"I hate guns," Renee said, again.

"We've got about six in the house," Adam said. Renee looked up at him, wide-eyed. Adam shrugged. "My dad and brother both hunt."

"But you don't," Renee said, more of an order than a question.

"Do I seem like the kind of son you want around if you're trying to kill something? They left me at home after I cried the first four times."

"Your family is *messed up*," Karen said.

Adam sighed. "Found out this morning Marty got a girl pregnant."

This stopped them both.

"At the super-Christian college?" Karen asked.

"Yep."

"People with really stiff morals are easier to tip over," Renee said. "That's what my mom always says."

"She's actually a black girl," Adam said. "Really, really pretty."

"Oh, man, their babies are going to be *beautiful*," Karen said, sounding almost disgusted. Marty's physical attractiveness had a small legend status, even in the grades that had followed his graduation.

"Or really ugly," Adam said. "Sometimes prettiness cancels itself out."

"What are they going to do?" Renee asked.

"What do you think they're going to do? Get married, have more pretty or ugly babies, preach at a church that thinks he's really boring but still likes to look at him in the pulpit every Sunday." He locked up the last handgun cage with Renee and they moved to the hunting bows. "Everything's easier when you're beautiful."

Karen and Renee both mm-hmmed in solemn

agreement. Neither of them had dated much, swearing they were waiting for college boys who'd "grown up a little". He didn't know how to tell them that the only college boy he knew in any depth was his own brother, and that didn't bode well for their romantic years ahead.

Karen looked at her phone. "Ten minutes till you're off, Adam," she said. "You want us to slow down so you don't have to talk to Wade?"

"I might as well get it over with," he said, handing the keys to Renee. The bows and arrows didn't have half as much security as the guns. "Thanks, though."

"See you at the party tonight?" Renee said, again shyly.

"Yeah. Why do you ask like that?"

She shrugged. "Just ... easier when you know someone you like's going to be there."

Adam felt a genuine ember of warmth in his gut. There was nothing carnal or wistful or indeed *wish*ful about Renee's words. She meant it as she said it, simply, easily. It was such an unexpected rush that he found himself, again, absurdly, with tears in his eyes.

"Yeah," he said, "I'll definitely be there."

He waved them goodbye and walked the length of the warehouse towards Wade's office, feeling the best moment he'd had all day. If not shaking off Marty's sting, then seeing how that might be possible as the day wore on. The feeling lasted nearly a full minute until Wade leaned out of his office door.

"Come in and sit down," Wade said.

"Do I have to?" Adam said.

"Afraid so." Wade looked surprisingly serious, so Adam slid inside. The office was so small he had to shut the door behind him before he could sit, and when he did, he and Wade were almost knee to knee, Wade's khakis bulging in a way that drew the horrified eye right to it.

Adam pressed himself as far back in his chair as he could. "What do you want, Wade? I don't have a lot of time."

"Yeah," Wade said, leaning back himself, putting his hands behind his head. The angle thrust the rest of him further forward. Adam had nowhere to put the left knee that Wade was now bumping. "That seems to be the problem with you lately, Thorn. Always somewhere to go. Always in a hurry to leave."

"What are you talking about? I'm on time for every shift. I never call in sick. I work every hour you put on the schedule–"

"Yeah, but you don't really do any more, do you? You don't go that extra mile. The giggle twins in there will work until that inventory is done, no matter what the schedule says."

Adam frowned. "You told me this company had no such thing as overtime."

"Oh, they won't be paid. They'll do it for knowledge of a job well done."

"They'll do it because they're afraid you'll fire them."

Wade cocked his head. "Aren't you?" He leaned forward and put his fingertips on Adam's knees, not in an obviously sexual way, in a way that could be explained later if necessary, but he still put them there when he didn't have to. "Because I've been wondering when I'm going to see you going that extra mile?"

Adam tried to squirm back, but there was no room. Wade's breath was a mixture of coffee and breakfast cereal. "I've got school," Adam said, swallowing, annoyed that he was. "I have to help my dad at the church."

"And that's all well and good," Wade said. He opened his fingertips so they brushed along the top of Adam's knees. "But we need to know we have your commitment here, too."

"Wade, that's not–"

"We value you. I mean, I know you and I joke around and have our laughs–"

"I don't laugh–"

"Seriously, Adam." He slapped his palms on Adam's thighs and kept them there, again in a way that could *almost* be written off as companionable, like an older gentleman encouraging the confidence of his younger charge.

But Wade's face was closer now, close enough for Adam to see the beads of sweat in his moustache. "This store doesn't want to lose you. *I* don't want to lose you."

Adam swallowed again. "Why would you lose me?"

"Budget cuts. The economy."

"The economy is improving."

"We're going to have to let people go, Adam. I don't want it to be you." Wade's hands hadn't moved, but somehow they felt heavier.

"I don't want it to be me either."

"I'm glad to hear you say that." Wade was still close, too close. Adam could smell his body now. Sweat, ageing cologne, something more intimate underneath that he didn't want to think about.

"They've been talking about reducing your hours," Wade breathed. "But I might be able to arrange something. If you can convince me you're the team player I think you are."

Adam saw that the bulge at Wade's crotch had shifted, was now unambiguously larger, like a third person in the office. Adam had fended off come-ons from men – and not a few women – before. He was young and big and blond and, if not in Marty's league of beauty, young and big and blond was more than enough for some people. There were men in the swimming pool locker room who seemed to have a hard time getting their trunks back on when Adam was changing near by. A woman on his paper route when he was thirteen had answered her door topless, not once, but three times, until he complained to his father. Even at the Christian summer camp, there was a counsellor whose private parts Adam had seen more often than normal averages would allow in the communal showers, the same counsellor who always "joked" about skinny-dipping.

Apart from the naked woman, it was always just on the edge of legality, could always be laughed off by the man, which no doubt Wade would do right now, right this very second–

"I'm not going to have sex with you, Wade," Adam said.

There was a flash in Wade's eyes, brief, fleeting, yet clear enough that for a second Adam thought Wade was about to grab him, force him, *rape* him in this overheated little office–

But then Wade leaned back. "You little bitch," he said, in a near-whisper.

"Are we done?" Adam said, trying not to let his voice shake, only partially succeeding.

"You come in here," Wade said, ignoring the question, "flashing that meaty little ass of yours, waving it in my face like a sow in heat, getting me to put my hands all over you–"

"Are you *kidding* me–"

"And now, and *now*!" Something weird happened to Wade's voice and it took a second before Adam realized he was forcing a laugh. "You *purposely* misunderstand a serious work conversation to make it seem like–" Wade rubbed the sweat from his moustache. "I don't know. Like I'm coming *on* to you, Thorn?"

"I can see your erection, Wade."

"Don't be disgusting!" Wade's hand immediately dropped to his crotch, covering it. "And now you're going to try and say that a little bit of *banter*, that we've *always* had, is somehow leading you to this bullshit idea that–"

"If you try to reduce my hours, I'm calling human resources."

Wade's face suddenly hardened, like a camera coming

into focus on a wasps' nest. "Too late, boyo. You're fired."

"What?"

"Pack your shit and get out."

"You can't–"

"Who are they going to believe, Thorn? You? You're a kid."

"You can't do this."

"Can, and did."

Adam felt a little ball of panic in his chest. "Wade, I need this job. My family, my *brother*–"

"Should've thought of that before you started telling lies."

"I haven't said anything. To anyone." He swallowed *again*. "Yet."

Wade raised an eyebrow.

Adam felt himself breathing. Where was he going with this? "Please," he said, and immediately hated himself for it.

"You begging me, Thorn?" Wade said with a sudden half-grin. He seemed to visibly relax, open his knees wider, his hand still at his crotch, dangling there with faux innocence.

"You can't... You can't do this to people, Wade."

"What people? I don't see any people here. Just a teenage pussy overestimating his own appeal. I got twenty years with this company. You think you can take *me* on? You think you can do that and win?"

"I could sue."

"And I'd be forced to tell the world how your faggotty

voraciousness made it nearly impossible to do my job in a safe working environment." And now Wade fully smiled. Adam wondered if there was anyone else in the world made so ugly by their smile. "What do you think the churchgoing folk of The House Upon The Rock would make of that?"

"You prick," Adam said, barely whistling it between his teeth.

"Could've been different, Thorn. We could've come to an understanding. But now–"

"I'll take the reduced hours," Adam said, hating himself more with every word. "I'll take a pay cut–"

Wade's crotch-level hand made a motion against the khaki. "What else are you willing to take?"

And for a second, a second he would relive for years to come, Adam found himself considering it. Would it really be so bad? Wade didn't look like someone who would ever take his time about anything, and if it was over quick, who would really be harmed...?

He would. The thought of Wade's hands on his bare skin alone gave him goosebumps, already felt like a violation, but if...

If he *deserved* this. (Did he?) If Wade had spotted in him – as he obviously had – that corruption at his heart, that little piece of unfixable brokenness–

It's not real love, Marty said.

We're just messing around, Enzo said.

Maybe it was all true.

Maybe this is what happened to people like him.

(People like *what*?)

"You think about it," Wade said. "If you come back in here for your shift on Monday, I'll know you made the right decision." He turned back to his computer. "Now get the fuck out of my office."

Adam left, clocking out on autopilot, not even saying goodbye to Karen and Renee, who were returning the scanning equipment. He left the warehouse and sat behind the wheel of his car, wondering what the hell had just happened. Had he *really* been given an ultimatum by his boss? Did that really happen to people?

His thumbs hovered over the letters on his phone. He typed, *I think I have to sleep with Wade to keep my job.*

Yuck... Angela replied, then, *Wait, are you serious?*

His phone rang immediately. "Call the police!" she said as soon as he answered.

"I need the money, Ange," he said. "I need the job."

"What happened?" He told her, and she said, "You are *not* going to sleep with Wade. He'd give you some seventies STD. Like herpes."

"No, of course not, but–"

"But nothing. He broke the law."

"Maybe... Maybe it didn't even happen. Maybe I read it wrong?"

Angela screamed in frustration so loud he had to pull the phone away from his ear. "Why am I the only one I know with any self-esteem?"

"You have wonderful parents."

"Look, where are you now?"

"I'm supposed to be going to Linus's."

"Come here first. I'm at work."

"But–"

"Remind yourself when I've got your back, Adam."

"Always."

"Damn right. Come now. Bring bulgogi."

She hung up. He held his phone for a long moment, then tossed it onto the passenger's seat, where it bumped the single red rose he'd bought this morning at the garden centre.

The red rose meant for someone today, meant for Linus, maybe. Meant for Linus, because who else? Idiot, he said to himself. You fucking idiot. The rose now just seemed embarrassingly corny, embarrassingly *gay*, something that deserved the scorn of a world where people like Wade could do whatever they wanted.

He refused to look at it as he drove away.

4

BECAUSE, PIZZAS

"Can I snap his wiener off?" Angela said, taking a bite of the bulgogi. "Like, with pliers?"

"I wouldn't even ask *you* to touch Wade on my behalf."

"It wouldn't *be* me. It'd be the pliers."

He could feel her watching him, waiting for whatever cues he'd give to tell her what he needed. He wasn't sure himself what the cues would be. First Marty and now Wade had knocked him so off-balance it was like those moments during running when he tripped but had not yet hit the ground, flailing like an ostrich for even the possibility of staying upright.

Where on earth had this day come from? And where was it headed?

Adam took another bite of lunch. Even in his upset, he had stopped off at the Korean barbecue place and picked up bulgogi. Angela's parents had made a concerted effort to keep Korean culture in her life and were faintly miffed that it often got reduced to holy-crap-this-bulgogi-is-awesome.

They were in the back room of Pizza Frome Heaven, one of Frome's lesser pizza places. It was in a small strip mall just slightly too far away from the larger strip mall where everyone usually went. But it did a good bulk deal and the pizza wasn't half bad. It wasn't necessarily half *good* either, but it would do for a "get-together" where everyone was going to be far more interested in the booze anyway.

"There's a fire up by the lake," he said. "I think it's near those cabins where Katherine van Leuwen was murdered."

"That poor girl," Angela said, seriously.

"I saw the smoke when I was driving here. I hope it doesn't screw up the get-together." He offered her the Styrofoam bowl. "Kimchi?"

"Ugh, no," she said, wrinkling her nose. "I don't know how you can eat that stuff."

"You're the one who's Korean."

"I'm sure I'm not the only Korean in the world who can't stand fermented cabbage. It smells like dogs humping. Seriously, Adam. Are you okay? Because I feel like killing someone."

Neither he nor Angela could honestly claim to have been through many terrible traumas after the car accident with her mom. They were, on the whole, fairly normal very-lower-middle-class kids in a rural suburb of the big megalopolis that curved around Puget Sound like a J. The

Thorns were a clergy family with airs and ambitions; the Darlingtons were farmers, for God's sake. Nobody had enough money to get into really interesting trouble, and nobody had the inclination for the more readily available trouble just anyone could afford.

Neither of them had ever done drugs – aside from trying a joint Angela had found in her parents' bedroom one night and to which she had proved embarrassingly allergic, requiring a shamefaced trip to the emergency room for the whole Darlington family, a good talking-to for Angela, and a promise to sweep the whole matter under the rug for Adam. Neither of them had ever caught STDs; Angela's mother gave Adam all the condoms he could ever want; and Angela had never got pregnant or even had a scare. She was way too smart for that.

They'd never had any run-ins with the police outside a speeding ticket (Adam) and a raided house party (Angela). Nobody they were close to had got cancer or MS or a tumour. No eating disorders, nothing requiring a psychiatrist (well, not a reputable one; Adam was sure his parents would have only been too happy to send him for a "cure" if they thought it was on the table, but even they knew not to push that one). The only real drama they had was Adam coming out to her, and Angela had done most of that for him anyway.

They'd just had life together. First kisses, last kisses, virginities lost, drinks tried, movies watched, classes shared, heartaches exchanged, world theories pontificated, gossip spread, uncontrollable laughter at nothing, polite dinners with respective families, mutual protection from bullies, gentle terrorizations of weak student teachers, early breakfasts every Friday before school at Denny's. All the stuff that counted. All the stuff that made the cement that stuck them together.

They'd been kids together. They'd been young teens together. They were growing up into adults together. It had been long enough and consistent enough that they'd gone past all boundaries. If she needed him, he'd be there instantly, no questions asked, and he knew she'd do the same. She was here now. They had their bulgogi. This is what a family was. Or should be.

"Do you remember the last year we went trick or treating?" he asked her.

"With the snow?" she said, surprised, but willing to go with it.

"With all that snow." Frome got heavy snowfall maybe once every six years and never as early as Halloween, but when they'd been in seventh grade – right at the outer barrier of trick or treating age – the snow had started and not stopped until there was a foot of it. Adam and Angela, dressed as Sookie Stackhouse and Bill Compton, not respectively, had to bury their costumes under a couple tons of heavy jackets, coats and scarves. "We got so much candy," he said.

"Because no little kids were out in the snow."

"And when we got back to your farm, my parents couldn't even get the car out to pick me up so I had to stay over."

Angela laughed, remembering the next bit. "And my mother–"

"Your mother–"

"Who makes two twelve-year-olds share a *foot bath*?"

"And all the eucalyptus she put in it."

"I still can't smell cough drops without thinking of the foot bath."

"I love your mom. That was when she told us about that racist Dutch Christmas thing."

"Zwarte Piet! Oh, my God! Even my hippie mother didn't think that was racist until she moved here."

"Yeah, I love your mom," he said again, which they both understood, maybe not even consciously, was another way of saying he loved Angela.

Speaking of which–

"There's something up, isn't there?" Adam asked. "Something you wanted to talk about?"

"Nothing like your day."

"That doesn't matter. Not even a little."

"In the face of Wade? I think you win." She stood and stretched, sniffing and then wincing at the front of her uniform. "I smell like onions."

"You always smell like onions after here. And it's not about winning. Quit changing the subject. What are you trying to avoid telling me?"

She gave him a side-eye, but thoughtfully. He could see her squinch her nose the way she never believed she did when she'd reached a decision.

"You know my aunt Johanna?"

"The one in Rotterdam? The professor?"

Angela nodded. "She wants me to go over there and be in that programme she set up at her university."

Adam creased his forehead. "Instead of college?"

"Instead of senior year."

Adam just stared while Angela crossed her arms and waited for it to sink in. This day showed no sign of stopping.

The faun does not see the incantation in time. He had not known she could do it in this form. Perhaps she did not know either, but away from the wreckage of the cabin – which he would not have time to repair, leaving a mystery this world would ponder and solve wrongly, as it always did – she begins patting a slow circle in the grass with her hand, the other held up towards the early afternoon sun.

Though worried, he has kept his distance, only intervening when the cabin nearly collapsed from the fire he also did not know she would be able to start. But he cannot approach too closely. He cannot enter her space or come within the reach of her arm.

She is the Queen. She must stand alone.

She turns faster now, and he can hear her saying something, though he cannot catch the words.

"My lady?" he asks, though he knows she won't hear him.

This form is cumbersome to him, all forms of the earth

are. It is an ancient one, the best he could find in the short time he had. It is too big for this world, too alien, too earthy.

But it is powerful.

She spins faster now, the knee-deep grass around her starting to bend as if under a whirlpool.

Though is she still the Queen? The soul that clings so blindly to her is surprisingly strong, and he knows she will be lost come sundown if he cannot find a way to–

And then he sees it.

And he is running.

Shouting, fruitlessly, "My lady, no!"

But the whirlpool of air rises from the earth, surrounding her in a funnel of dust and grass and the timothy hay that grows wild in these fields–

He is too late. The funnel collapses as he arrives, and she is gone.

She is gone.

She will not have gone far, but in this wilderness, both of trees and houses, even near by is far enough. How will he find her? How will he find her in time?

There is nothing for it, no time to even berate himself for his stupidity. The Queen must be found and, somehow, saved before the sun sets or she will die.

And if she dies, then so does the faun, for she is the boundary, the wall between these worlds.

If she dies, so do they all.

He begins to run towards the forest of houses. He hopes all he will have to do is listen for the screams.

Angela Darlington. The girl born in Seoul with an adoptive mother from the Netherlands and a father with a completely English name. Who all lived on a farm in Frome, Washington, an actual farm, with actual animals, actual sheep that got sold to slaughter – a topic Angela kept quiet about as it wouldn't have gone down well with the vegetarians at school. They were, in short, about as American as you could be.

But not, of course, the kind of Americans certain other kinds of Americans thought were American.

"She's Dutch, you say?" Big Brian Thorn would ask occasionally about Angela's mother, even though he couldn't possibly have forgotten in the previous decade. "They're a funny people, the Dutch." He'd give the newspaper he was reading a disapproving shake. "Liberal about everything. Marijuana. Prostitution."

"The Darlingtons don't do any of that," Adam would answer. "Though I think they probably did vote for all the Clintons."

"I'm just saying, the tendency is there. Towards a relative look at the world, where you can eventually talk yourself into thinking that pretty much anything at all is okay."

"Oh, come on, Brian," his mother said this particular time, filling in a job application on her laptop. "You like Angela."

"I *do* like Angela," his father answered. "I'm just saying it's hard to deprogramme from that stuff. I don't know how many times we've invited them to church." He glanced over at Adam. "You could be a real witness to that girl."

"I don't even understand what they mean by the verb," Angela said to him whenever he brought it up. "Wouldn't *I* be the witness, watching you tell me about it?"

"It's more like I'm giving you a witness statement."

"Like you saw God committing a crime?"

"I'm supposed to be offering my *own* witness on what Christ has done for me."

"Made you gay and put you in the best possible family for dealing with that? At least He has a sense of humour."

"Maybe I'm meant to witness to my family?"

"How's that working out?"

"We've all silently agreed to disagree."

But Adam's parents did like her. That was true. They liked her manners around them, liked how hard she worked on her farm and at the pizza place without ever seeming to complain. They liked her enough that Adam was sure they still held out the hope he'd one day just marry her, whatever sexual agreement they had to work out to do it.

They didn't know Angela was fluid enough to sometimes flow to girls. Particularly girls with kissable lips, the thinness of Angela's own the sole physical feature she regularly complained about.

"I'll bet Dutch people have really thin lips," he said now, in the back room of Pizza Frome Heaven.

And again, she knew him well enough not to even blink at the non sequitur. "Like their really tall bodies?"

"You'd be very short if you went. Short*er*."

"You're tall, Adam. I know your ways and tempers. I know when to feed you and what your mating calls sound like."

"It's all about rolling into a ball when we want to rut."

"Don't I know it."

"What if I need you here to be my guide for the clinically short?"

"You'll do fine without me."

"I won't," he said.

"No, probably, and I won't be fine without you."

"It'll be like losing a minor limb. A hand or something."

"An ear."

"My hair."

"Oh, you'll be losing that soon enough. I've seen your dad."

Then she waited, waited to see how he would *really* take it.

He patted the seat next to him. She came over and sat down. They leaned side by side against each other.

"When do you leave?" he asked. He was so much taller than her he could rest his left cheek all the way across the top of her head.

"Week from Tuesday," she said, sounding sadder than he wanted.

"Wow. Will you come back for Christmas?"

"I want to, but my mom is already talking about Christmas in Rotterdam."

"Zwarte Piet," Adam said.

"Maybe I can start a protest movement or something."

They didn't move as Angela's shift manager came in, a tall black senior called Emery from their school who was essentially raising his younger brothers as their mother slowly died of dementia. "Hey, Adam," he said.

"Hey, Emery, how's your mom?"

"Oh, you know. No worse this week at least."

"Good."

Emery glanced at Angela. "Lunch rush is coming. I'm going to need you back."

Angela nodded. "Give me a minute, though."

Emery shook his head affectionately at her and Adam. "Weirdest couple I know." He left them, holding up his fingers to say she could have two more minutes.

"You going to miss me?" Angela asked.

"Are you kidding?"

"Yeah. You are."

"But I know you wouldn't go if you didn't want to."

And even though he couldn't see her face, he could practically *feel* her smiling. "Europe, Adam. I'll be living in *Europe*. For a whole year." She turned to him. "You have to find a way to visit."

"With what money? I don't have a job any more."

"Oho, *that* story isn't even close to being finished. You'll come to Rotterdam with the money you win from the sexual harassment suit against Wade."

"Because my parents would totally support *that* public debacle."

She got up and stood in front of him. They were finally at matching heights and she rested her forehead against his own. "I'll sure as hell miss you, Adam Thorn."

"You won't have a shortage of super-tall Dutch people to remind you of me."

Her eyes lit up. "And maybe one of them will be *straight*."

"Not according to what I've heard about the Dutch."

She play-slapped him. "My mom is Dutch."

"Do you think we would have dated?"

She leaned down and looked into his eyes, so closely their eyelashes were almost touching. "I think we would have dated and married and made babies of average height. And then divorced when you realized you were gay."

"I'm always gay?"

"In every universe."

"That makes sense. Are you always short?"

"Except in the universes where I'm Beyoncé."

"In some universes, we're *all* Beyoncé."

The town is not large, but even so. The faun repeatedly smells the air, hoping for some scent of her, but only after much frustration does he realize he's been sniffing for his Queen.

When, of course, at the moment, she is someone else entirely.

He curses his foolishness and pulls his mind back to the body of the dead girl – though calling it a "body" is wrong. It is not exactly a spirit either, not in the way the faun knows spirits. The jealous, capricious spirits of the lake, for example, who sometimes chafe under the rule of the Queen. Would they fight to keep her? the faun wonders. Even if losing her meant their own destruction? An eternity of rule is perhaps an eternity too long for some.

No, surely not. They loved the Queen. And if they did not, they feared her, which is how it should be, how it always had been.

He would not allow her reign to end. He would not.

And the not-quite-spirit that had caught her had her own scent. One of this world, the world she had left. It had been a violent passage out of it, to be sure, but not the first that had been made through the lake, nor the first that had passed near the Queen.

But this spirit had refused. She had not known what or how she was refusing, but she had felt a pearl of blood calling to her – he knew, for he had smelled it, too, the scent of another's destiny on the day it changed itself – and she had clearly decided to refuse her own. In that moment of refusal, she had turned the Queen's head–

And the Queen had been caught and today, somehow, made flesh. When that happened, a spirit was only given until sundown to walk this earth one last time. Only until sundown.

He remembers the spirit, remembers her scent at the cabin.

He closes his eyes and inhales deeply again.

There. There she is.

He moves through the town at a speed unseen by its citizens, though not unfelt. There is gooseflesh at his passing, a shiver down the spine, perhaps a shiver that moves all the way to the loins – he is in the form of a faun after all, rude, lusty, recognized (wrongly) as a god, (rightly) as a fertility assist. There will be more than one baby conceived here this afternoon.

But these are only fleeting thoughts as he steps between the moments and seconds of these creatures' odd and fractious little lives. He can scent her. There is a twist of her on the breeze, braiding itself in a helix too faint for the noses of all but the most attentive hounds and the faun himself.

He can sense she has stopped somewhere. She grows larger in the horizon of his senses. And beyond her–

Beyond her, there is a wall of scents like hers.

She has found her home. She has found her family.

The faun begins to move faster.

She has found her home. The home of this body, the family of it. There is such a pull here, strands of sorrow leaking into the air so dark and malevolent it's a wonder these creatures can't see them, see how they poison this house.

"How they will be its death," she says, aloud.

Then she wonders, Am I that death? Is that how it shall happen?

She stands before a neglected front yard. Grass grows high over a derelict mower in one corner. Abandoned baby toys – whose? what baby's? does she know? she does not – hide among the browning lawn. A chain-link fence surrounds it, so low she steps over it in one hitched stride, less keeping anything in than simply marking the space as owned. There is evidence of a dog – a chain, a collar – but Victor, the boyfriend before Tony, had taken a dislike to it, a mutt called Karl, and Karl had vanished one night. No proper explanation had been forthcoming from Victor.

"And yet I did not leave," she says, bothered, unsettled.

She can feel the wound in her heart from Victor, one

he kept fresh and bleeding, one in which he had placed a hook that kept her tethered to him. She was terrified of him. She could not leave him.

Until she did.

Oh, the day of it, the day she had left Victor. She had said her unhappiness. She had turned down the drugs he offered to make her stay. She had not blinked at the threats he made. She didn't know why, that day of all days, but he railed and screamed and threatened and all she had seen was his fear that she was leaving him, leaving him alone with the demon in his veins that would surely kill him as it would surely kill her.

And then he had wept. And she had seen through it. The tears weren't real. He was manipulating her. Again. And if they weren't real, nothing else was real, nothing but his fear.

And that gave her the power.

"So I shut the door," she says. *And she had. She had walked Victor to the doorway, an almost kind hand on his back, and she had guided him out the front door – this door, here, the one before her now – and he had turned and said "Katie?" and she had just...*

Shut the door.

For a moment, she had been strong. For a moment, she had trembled from that strength. For a moment, anything was possible, a future, a way to make it better, to make it right, to step out of this rut, out of these weights that clung to her like bricks in her pockets. For almost an entire evening, there was possibility.

Then Tony came over. With a baggie. Four months later, he murdered her.

But there had been the moment when she shut that door.

There will always be that moment.

That same door that opens before her now.

The heavy woman behind it looks at her, eyes opening so wide as to seem almost painful. But then those eyes shut and the woman drops to her doorstep, in a faint.

"Mother?" says the Queen.

Adam and Angela had lost their virginities within a month of each other, though not by design. She'd lost hers, after much deliberation, with Kurt Miller, he of the peach fuzz moustache and pimply chin. She liked him but didn't love him, which she thought was the perfect combination.

"That way I can actually have the experience with a decent guy and see what it might be like."

"That's very idealistic," Adam had said.

"Well," she replied, "I *am* young."

He'd waited up half the night for her call, his phone on silent under the covers. There'd been no lying necessary to cover for her parents. Mrs Darlington knew where Angela was, though wouldn't know what had happened until it was over with. Adam had spent a surprisingly large portion of the evening wondering what that must be like.

His phone lit up and he answered immediately. "How was it?"

"His penis wasn't porn ready. At all."

Adam laughed, as he knew he was intended to, and then he asked, also as he knew he was intended to, "How was it really?"

And he listened to her while she cried. "Do I need to kill him?" he said, his voice serious.

"No," she said, quickly. "Not at all. It was just … so much *work* for really not very much. And it hurt. I mean, Jesus, Adam, why does no one tell you that? It hurts."

"I've heard it hurts for guys, too."

"It didn't hurt Kurt."

"Not what I meant."

"Oh. Well, still. It hurt. And it was weird. And his dick looked like a mushroom. Not even a very big one."

"I know. We have gym together."

"Well, why didn't you *say*?"

"It's not as if they don't change shape, Angela."

"His didn't. Not very much. Poor Kurt."

"Poor Angela."

"I don't think I could have taken much more size, frankly. Not the first time. Thank God it was so *fast*."

"Are you really okay? Are these jokes to cover sadness?"

"Yeah, they are."

"Need me to sneak out?"

"You can't sneak out. Your mom has the house alarmed."

"This is true."

"I was just… I mean, I didn't exactly have my expectations high–"

"You did a little."

"Yeah. Don't you?"

"Yeah. Like the kiss in *Brokeback Mountain*."

"It's not gonna be like that."

"I know. Are you seriously okay?"

She blew out her breath. "I'm a little sticky."

"Was Kurt nice?"

"Really nice. I didn't expect him to be. Lousy kisser, but I knew that going in. I can say this, though, Adam. The touches... The touches are something else. A body next to yours and all that skin, like *miles* of skin, you never think anyone else would have that much skin and... The way it *smells*, like a kiss but so much darker. It was awkward and it was kind of horrible and it hurt and I bled and it was short, but there were parts of it..."

"Yeah."

"It's gotta get better. Doesn't it?"

"That's what people say."

He heard her cry a little bit more. "I'm really tired," she said, "and my contacts have gone all dry."

"Call me in the morning."

"Before I call Kurt, that's for sure."

She never dated Kurt. He wasn't a bad guy, he didn't spread anything around. Angela forever referred to it as an "anthropological excursion", one she remembered fondly but more for the scientific notes she'd gathered than for the experience itself.

Notes that he found unconvincing in their ongoing debate the next day about his own virginity loss. "There are levels if you're a boy," he'd argued. "Especially one who likes other boys."

"There are levels for girls, too."

"You can say that all you want, but the world thinks your virginity is one thing and one thing only."

"Which is completely arbitrary and unfair."

"Agreed, but when do *you* think you lost your virginity?"

"Last night... Oh."

"Yeah. Oh. So when do I lose mine? Is a handjob enough?"

"When did you get a handjob?"

"Ah, see, now that's another question. What if I just *give* one?"

"When did you *give* a handjob?"

He didn't answer.

"You haven't, have you?" Angela said, though it came out less a question than an assertion.

"You mean aside from to myself?"

"There's also a word the entire world gives *that*."

"Well, when would I have had the chance?"

And this was true. Compared to teens in movies and books and on TV, he and Angela weren't especially oversexed throughout most of early high school. Which was probably just as well, as everyone around them – and them, too – was too busy actually growing into their bodies to want very much to show them naked to anyone else.

It was harder for Adam due to lack of availables.

Still, Linus was somehow the fourth person he'd had sex with, Enzo the second. A fumble with a sweetly geeky and astonishingly pale guy named Larry in his teen group at the church had been between them. That was after a music rehearsal when Big Brian Thorn had invited the teen choir over to the house for fellowship. Adam found Larry crying in his bedroom. Seven minutes and an ejaculation later, Larry was crying again, but for different reasons: gratitude and guilt. Larry had studiously avoided him at church ever since, though to be honest, it had all been so unexpected, Adam occasionally forgot it had ever happened.

He never forgot his actual virginity loss, though.

Philip Matheson, a name almost as English as Angela Darlington. He was a junior when Adam was finishing his freshman year, though the age difference was only eighteen months, and he was a rare member of the Frome High School Cross-Country Team who was taller than Adam. Broader, too, but like a lot of fairly massive people, quite shy with it. They only started talking because Philip – never Phil, never – was glad to have someone he could hide behind during the team photo.

"We both should have really been swimmers," Philip had said, that day outside the school, the short members of the team holding the school banner down front.

"I hate swimming," Adam said. "Though my feet are flat enough."

"It'd be nice if you could always get a pool to yourself. I only really like a sport you can do completely alone."

133

At that, Adam had looked up at him, the first person in a long, long time he could actually look up *at*. Philip had darker hair than Adam, darker stubble – though Adam still barely had anything that could pass for stubble at all, to be fair – and he blushed when Adam caught his eye, actually *blushed*.

Three months later, at a party much like tonight's at Philip's own house, Philip had a beer, Adam had a beer, Philip had another, Adam had another, and out by the indoor pool Philip's father had built, Philip had completely avoided looking Adam in the face when he said, "Wouldn't it be funny if we, like, kissed?"

The next ninety-three minutes that Adam waited for the party to clear while calculating how worth it the damage would be from parents who had expressly forbidden he stay over with "this friend we haven't met", were the longest ninety-three minutes of his life.

"Is it okay if I haven't kissed anyone before?" Adam had asked, finally up in Philip's bedroom.

"Anyone at all?" Philip said. "Or just another guy?"

"Anyone at all. Sorry."

"Whoa. Really, whoa." And Philip had kissed him. He tasted of beer and tongue and beery tongue and smelled of sweat and of faint cologne and of boy. Just that, he smelled of another boy, so much that the ache in Adam's body was almost palpable and he couldn't keep from shaking. Then Philip had started unbuttoning Adam's shirt and every die was cast. Adam was so stunned, he didn't actually move until Philip had undressed him completely, with the strange intent of someone who was, by God, going to finish a job he had started, lest he notice what he was doing and stop. When Adam was finally completely naked – and Philip still completely not – Philip had run fingers down the flesh of Adam's arms and said, "There." Just, "There."

This was the moment Adam always remembered, even more than that first incredible kiss: the first time being naked and, well, *hard* in front of someone else. There was no going back from this, no joke that would cover it, there was only this moment when someone was actually looking at it, at *him*, was actually reaching out to touch it, take it in their hand, and that … that was the impossible going right ahead and happening.

There was naked and then there was *naked*.

"There," Philip said.

Everything was new. Everything was a first. He'd seen it all on porn, obviously, but Philip had been hairier than that in surprising places, everything less perfect, but that was so much more exciting than perfect could ever, ever be. And the skin. Angela was so right about the skin that Adam couldn't stop looking, even when they were kissing, until Philip had put up a gentle hand and closed his eyes. "You're staring," he'd whispered.

"Sorry."

"Stop apologizing."

"Sorry."

"It really is your first time, isn't it?" Philip had smiled back then leaned away into the light so that Adam could take a long, long look, just seeing everything. Philip wasn't the most beautiful guy in the whole wide world, no, but right then, he was the most beautiful thing Adam had ever seen. Ever seen all of.

"I'm sorry I'm a little hefty," Adam said.

"*I'm* not."

They'd carried on, but looking back and knowing more, Adam couldn't imagine the experience had been all that interesting for Philip, as Adam had mostly just lain there, half in shocked inexperience, half trying not to let it finish at every desperate second.

Then Philip had whispered a request in his ear. "Can I…" was all he got out, as if too embarrassed to say the verb.

"I've never done that either."

"That's okay then–"

"But yeah. Yes."

"Are you sure?"

"Yes."

"Are you *sure*?"

"I think so."

Philip had looked him in the eye. "I'll go slow," he said, and put on a condom.

He went slow. It didn't help.

"I can stop any time," Philip said.

"Can you just … not move for a second?"

"Of course. It always hurts like this first time."

"Then why do people do it?" Adam managed to say.

"Because wait for it. Just wait."

Adam waited. The initial pain subsided. It grew tolerable. Then it grew completely remarkable. Physically, sure, but mentally, too. They were face to face still, and Adam could see the ferocious concentration Philip was putting himself through, wondered if he was thinking the same thing as Adam. *I am having sex. I'm having actual sex with an actual man.*

I am having sex.

I am having sex.

He said embarrassing sex things. He said them probably quite loudly. But Philip did, too. And when they were done, and they were still together, still connected, before they even started cleaning up, Philip had kissed him again, holding his lips and tongue for a long, long moment, then saying, "I wish we'd done this sooner."

Because it turned out Philip, like Enzo, like Angela for that matter, was about to move away. They'd never got together again. They'd texted a few times, but mostly it was Philip wishing him well and saying goodbye in various ways, as he took off for a senior year in Omaha. Adam was disappointed, of course, but also smart enough to know it might never have happened if Philip hadn't been going. Would he have risked it? Would he have said nothing at all, leaving Adam quite clueless?

But it had happened. Twenty-seven days after Angela. And he'd called her at three o'clock that morning, sitting on the edge of the bathtub in Philip's house, feeling tired, sore, spent, and different, different, different.

"Oh, my God," Angela had sleepily whispered.

"I know," he'd whispered back.

"Oh, my God."

"I *know*."

"Are you okay?"

"My parents are going to murder me and I don't even care. That's how okay I am."

"I have so many questions."

"Tomorrow."

"Like ... *so* many."

His parents didn't quite murder him, but he'd been grounded for the next month and made to clean the church every single Wednesday of that summer. And Angela had asked many, many, many, many questions, most of them eye-wateringly anatomical.

"I didn't ask this much about Kurt."

"Well, you totally could."

"You're not taking my hint here."

"Oh, you love me, and you know it."

And he did. Love her. With all his aching heart.

The faun finds her kneeling by the body of a large woman. He thinks his way into the woman's chest and finds a heart still beating – albeit in a flawed, laborious way that can surely not be long for this world.

"Wake up, Mom," he hears his Queen say. "It's your Katie."

He has already erased the memories of those he's passed: the neighbours of this house; the man who'd been driving by, ready to throw a newspaper over the short fence; the two little girls with dirty faces who had stopped their own argument – about something called "mango candy lip dazzle" – and stared at him as he approached, neither of them screaming, not just yet. He held his hands over their eyes, and returned them to their dazzle.

And now here is his Queen, kneeling over her mother, when it is the Queen who is the Mother, the Mother of them all—

He sees her look around at the house beyond the

darkened doorway where the woman fainted. "I know this place."

She stands, leaving the woman behind, entering the house. The faun steps over the large woman, searching her mind, finding the right things to erase. He ducks under the lintel of the door – he is far too tall to be comfortable inside any dwelling these creatures make for themselves – and he follows the Queen in a crouch. The house smells not of death, like the cabin did, but of grief, a cold and heavy scent that slows him down, even in the short entryway.

The house is quiet. No one else is at home, though the unconscious woman is not the only one who resides here. He can smell an older man and two other younger women who were here this morning, their scents lingering like ghosts walking up and down these rooms.

The spirit's smell has components of these, as they have components of hers. The physical ties of families.

But he stops as he smells that the grief here works two ways. They feel the grief of her loss. But her grief is here as well. There was loss before her loss. There was empti-ness, which is the same as loss.

Blinking in this corporeal body, he moves on.

He finds her in front of a hearth, though no fire has been lit there for some months. On the mantel above, there are photographs.

There are photographs of her.

"What are you smiling about?" Angela said, poking her head into the back room.

"I was just remembering Kurt Miller," Adam said.

"Sweet guy. I was sad when he moved away."

"Not sad enough to be friends on social media."

"I'm not desperate."

"I was thinking of Philip Matheson, too."

"The boy who took Adam's flower." She nodded, understanding. "Someone's looking for physical consolation."

"Might help wash Wade off me."

She sat down next to him again. "I've got to get back on the floor, but... It's okay to not be okay, you know."

"I know. I'm happy for you. But selfish enough to be sad for me."

"And Wade?"

"I'm not sad for him at all."

"Adam–"

"I can't lose my job. Paying for college was going to be iffy anyway–"

His phone buzzed. A text from Marty. Angela read it with him over his shoulder. *You do not stay angry forever but delight to show mercy, Micah 7:18.*

"Who quotes Micah?" Adam said.

"And who's the 'you' in that sentence?" Angela said.

"He's saying sorry. I think? Maybe? He believes some awful shit, but at heart, he's not the worst person I know."

Angela sighed. "Go to Linus. Wash Wade off. Get some loving. I'll see you tonight."

"For a going-away party that suddenly has more people going away?"

"We can just eat all three dozen pizzas over at my house if you want."

Adam grinned at her, sadly.

She grinned back, sadly, too. "You can't miss me yet. Now, seriously, go. We'll figure this shit out, but you've got Linus waiting." And then she said something he knew her mother had always said to her. "Never pass up the chance to be kissing someone. It's the worst kind of regret."

*She reaches out to touch the photographs, but stops short.
"This is me," she hears herself whispering, amazed. "This
is who I was."*

*This is who she was, thinks the Queen, and for a
moment the separation is clear, for a moment she can
almost step behind this body and see it, looking at the
photos of itself. She feels her own power, restless, churning, the power of the waters of the world, the power that
answers to the moon and the moon alone, the power that
could level this house, destroy this body, destroy this
town, if such a thing were ever to be allowed again–*

*"What–?" says the Queen in her own voice. "How
have I–?"*

*And this fleeting spirit, this weak, fleeting spirit
that should have no hold on her, this spirit surrounds
her again, binds her, seems even unaware of her presence
except as a vehicle for itself, and the Queen forgets, as
she steps back into the body that welcomes her.*

Her glance moves from photo to photo. There are none of her with the hands that killed her. None showing the bruises around her throat.

"I was unhappy here," she says. And from that unhappiness she went out and found, not happiness, but numbness, which is what she thought her only option was.

She knows why she came here. It is home. It drew her. Even as Tony's hands were choking her, even as she could feel the blood boiling in her temples in a way that spoke only of irreversible damage, even when she woke for the last few seconds of her life in the silt of the lake, drowning, her lungs filled, even then, she thought of home. She thought of here.

She realizes her mistake.

"This was my home," she says, "but it is not my home now."

The faun barely has time to get out of her way as she turns and leaves, still not seeing him–

(Though for a moment there, for a moment–)

She steps past him, back out the front door, over the woman–

The woman now waking–

"Katie?" asks the woman, certain she is dreaming.

"Katie is dead," says his Queen, not looking back, heading out into the world.

The faun has no choice but to follow.

5

LINUS AT
2 O'CLOCK

Second shower of the day. Adam stood under the spray in Linus's bathroom, breathing in the steam, washing the smell of the Evil International Mega-Conglomerate, the smell of Wade's office, the smell of *Wade* – though, to be fair, also the smell of pizza and bulgogi – out of his hair.

Linus poked his head around the shower curtain, his glasses immediately steaming up. "You okay in here?"

"Yeah," Adam said.

"Angela's right, you know," Linus said, taking off his glasses, blinking his big, half-blind eyes in a way that Adam found impossibly adorable. "You have to report him."

"Can we talk about it another time?"

"Sure."

"It's just," Adam said, "I'm naked and you're too cute for me to believe right now."

Linus smiled his gleaming, toothy smile that looked all Broadway but had actually happened naturally, no braces ever needed. "Not so bad yourself," he said. "In a blurry, steamy way. You sure you don't want company?"

"Not yet, but soon." Adam let the water run off his shoulders and down his pale belly, already a little plump. A lifetime of negotiating with it beckoned. "Angela's going to spend senior year in Holland in a programme her aunt runs."

Linus's mouth opened in surprise. "*You've* had a busy morning."

"In one amazing way I'm really happy for her."

"And in another?"

Adam looked up from the spray and the steam into Linus's still-blinking eyes. "Maybe don't move away any time soon?"

"Not planning on it."

"Good. And I'll be in Frome for the rest of my life, I think, so, you know, if either of you ever want to visit–"

"You'll get out. We all will. Every gay has to have their years in a huge coastal city. It's like a law."

Adam just breathed again. "I'm kinda using up all your hot water."

"We're in the rainiest state in the Union. We'll struggle through."

"Is there something wrong with me, Linus?"

"Lack of willingness to manscape?"

"Ugh, no, I hate that stuff. I'm not Barbie."

"No, you're really, really not Barbie."

"I'm serious."

"And a little self-pitying."

"Sorry."

"Forgiven. You've had a remarkably shit day and it's only two o'clock," Linus said. "Look, there's nothing more wrong with you than there is with anyone else. And nothing so wrong that I don't spend all my time thinking about great big ungroomed naked you wasting hot water in my shower while my parents are out playing softball."

Adam smiled, slightly, then leaned forward and gave Linus a wet kiss.

"Nothing so wrong," Linus said, "that I wasn't able to fall in love with you."

Adam used the tip of his tongue to touch the faint coffee taste Linus always left on his lips and said, "I love you, too."

The girl they have found is clearly under the influence of a drug. Her eyes are open, she is breathing, but she sees neither the Queen nor the faun as they approach the sofa where she lies.

"You are Sarah," the Queen says to her, not a greeting, a fact.

The girl hears this – or some form of it – and her eyes swim to the Queen, though who could say what she actually sees?

The Queen has led the faun on an unerring straight line that took notice of no boundary or landscape. They crossed roads and houses, only going around an obstacle when going through it would have taken too much time. All this in broad daylight, on a day when these creatures were mostly at their leisure. There are still memories upon memories he needed to erase. He begins to despair. What can it matter if they see? If he can't save the Queen, all is lost anyway.

They came to a house. This house. One that smells of a

sickness so powerful the faun had to force himself to go inside.

"You are Sarah," the Queen says again, kneeling in front of the sofa, taking the hand of the girl–

And unexpectedly, from nowhere, the faun sees a chance.

She feels such love for this girl, it almost makes her stumble. Sarah. This person, this friend, this home–

She had known after seeing her mother, after returning to that place that had offered silences or screaming but little in between, a place where more than one of her mother's boyfriends had put hands on her over the years, a place where – after she told her mother about the first boyfriend who did so – her mother had beaten her for a liar. These images come to her now in a kind of swimming clarity. Because she was inside it all those years, it had still somehow always looked like home.

It has taken death to finally see it for what it was. The mouth of a predator.

But here, this house, this girl, this Sarah, even seen from the outside, even from beyond the borders of the sickness and blindness that bind her here–

This, this is her home. This is where love had been found, even refuge when necessary. Oh, that she had been able to see it sooner. Maybe she could have saved her friend. Maybe she could have saved herself.

The Queen reaches forward, takes Sarah's hand.

Sarah wakes. And sees the Queen.

Linus Bertulis, a Lithuanian name, even though his ancestors had been in America longer than the Thorns. Linus Bertulis, at the top of all the College Prep classes, taking half his subjects at the local university extension because he was so far ahead of anyone else. Linus Bertulis, who Adam wanted to love so much it almost physically hurt.

Linus was cute, and that was a fact. He was a nerd, like Renee and Karen said, but nerdiness – like a big nose, like a belly – was never any barrier to cuteness. He wore black-rimmed glasses, had a thick swoop of brown hair that was already showing signs of handsome recession, and dressed with an old-fashioned formality that mostly, but not always, stopped just short of a bow tie.

Adam would never be able to introduce Linus to his parents. He was polite, friendly, smiley, and would raise so many suspicions, Adam's mom and dad would probably send Adam on a year-long mission trip to Turkmenistan just to get him out of town until graduation.

Linus liked the same horror movies Adam and Angela did, almost exclusively read three-inch thick fantasies with sexy elves on the covers, while also somehow being a competitive ballroom dancer. Seriously. He danced with an Italian girl called Marta and they sometimes even won things. It also meant that under the vintage blazers and tailored trousers, he had an absolutely extraordinary butt. Just extraordinary. Adam frequently marvelled at it when he held it in his hands.

Like now.

"I thought we were going to eat first," Linus said, as they lay on his bed.

"I had bulgogi. Your butt is extraordinary."

"If you don't got core strength, you ain't a ballroom dancer."

"You have more muscles than I do. Like, by a lot."

"It's always a surprise to the boys in PE. But *you* can run sixteen miles at a stretch if you have to."

"Which has given me thighs but no butt."

"Your thighs could snap one of my arms off, though."

"They should add that to ballroom competitions. Thigh clamping."

"I have no idea where this train of thought is heading, Adam," Linus said, but he was smiling.

Linus, to Adam's astonishment, had made the first move. Like damn near everyone else in Frome, they'd known each other at least distantly since about the second grade, but they'd hung out with different crowds. If you could call Angela a "crowd". Defying stereotype, Linus was in chess club but not drama club, though he did have about a zillion girl best friends. He also had a name that people over forty seemed to find amusing but that other teenagers took in their stride. You had to, in a world of Briannas and Jaydens, but also because of how Linus wore it. If anyone was going to carry off the name Linus in a small town, it was Linus.

Linus never even had to come out. As a sophomore, he took a boy – from another school, but a boy nonetheless – to the Junior Prom (having charmed his way into a ticket) and the only person at Frome High who even batted an eyelid was FHS's very Christian front office secretary, who wrote a note to Linus's parents, who in turn wrote a note back explaining in great detail how she and the school district would be sued if she ever tried to discriminate against their son again.

This was a world, an intoxicating and possible world, which Adam saw as if through a veil, unreachable. Desperately close, but impossibly far... Because the Junior Prom *had* caused a (very) minor furore among the evangelical preachers of Frome, of which there were a fair number. It was Big Brian Thorn, though – eyeing as ever the crowds at The Ark of Life – who saw an opening in staking out a position extreme enough to get people's attention. For ninety minutes Adam sat through a sermon that could only have been directed at him, though no one in the entire building, not least his father, would admit it. "I would sit outside that dance in sackcloth and cover myself in manure if that were my child." He really said that. Which probably shouldn't have made Adam think that, in order to sit outside in protest, his father would have had to let him go to the dance with a boy in the first place. Still, the car ride home had been particularly silent.

It was also the main reason (of many) Adam's parents didn't know how Linus existed in Adam's life. Fortunately, they'd never quite caught Linus's name, and God bless Angela for months of cover stories.

Linus had found Adam alone in a Red Robin, where Angela was coming to meet him from the farm. It was only a few weeks after Enzo had declared an annulment of their relationship. Which was an especially difficult way to be broken up with, as now Adam was in the position of mourning something that had allegedly never been.

"You all right?" Linus had asked out of nowhere. Adam hadn't even seen him come in. He'd sat facing away from the restaurant with a raspberry lemonade, in a kind of limbo of non-movement until Linus was suddenly across the table from him. "You look a little upset. Lost, kind of."

"Yeah, I'm okay," Adam had said, a little taken aback that a boy was speaking to him like this, when they were only ever phrases he heard from girls or himself. "Waiting for someone."

"Angela Darlington?"

Adam was surprised, as he always was, when someone knew even a minor fact about him. "Yeah," he said.

"Anything you want to talk about before she gets here?" Linus said, kindly. "You really don't look very happy."

"We don't even know each other, Linus."

Linus hesitated, but Adam saw him decide to push ahead. "I think maybe we do. Don't you?"

Adam wondered at the depth of this, how far down into the still pond this stone had been meant to fall. Linus gave him a moment and glanced around the restaurant, at the brass rails, the brown shiny leather of the booths slick with the accumulated grease of a thousand nights of burgers and fries, checking that they couldn't be overheard. He leaned closer to Adam, his face concerned, his voice gentle. "I know why you're sad. I know why you're afraid."

"I'm not afraid."

"Liar," he said, still gentle. "*I'm* afraid. Every day. And if it's that hard for me—"

"Then how hard must it be for pathetic Adam Thorn?" Adam's voice had some heat in it.

"Well," Linus said, "yes. Except the pathetic part. We don't pick our families. Or the sermons they preach."

Adam winced. "Oh, God, you know about that?"

"You honestly think social media would have kept me in ignorance?" He made a dismissive hand. "It passed in a week, but the whole time, all I thought about was how *you* were taking it."

"Linus—"

"And we *also*," he pressed on, "don't pick who we fall for. We don't make them turn out to be complete dickheads."

Adam's stomach was tumbling with how much Linus

knew and how he'd found it all out (it would turn out he knew as much as nearly everyone else in the school, which was a lot, but it also turned out that – in that unreachable, possible world – most of them actually liked Adam or at least didn't actively wish him harm, so they'd given his sorrow some space; when Adam thought about it now, it still made his head swim, still made him blush, still made him wish he could crawl under a blanket and die there forever) – but looking at Linus, he saw no malice, no gossip, saw instead someone who might actually know. He'd heard once that the only people who could effectively treat the trauma of surviving an airplane crash were other survivors of airplane crashes. You could only instinctively trust someone who had been there, who had seen it first-hand.

Then Linus – and he actually did this, he really actually did – reached across the table and put his hand on Adam's, a strangely old-fashioned gesture that went with everything else strangely old-fashioned about Linus Bertulis.

"No," he said, "I guess we don't really know each other. But maybe…"

He fell silent. Adam could feel himself holding his breath. "I'm kind of waiting for Angela here," he said.

Linus smiled again. "Angela is a bit awesome."

"She is."

"And if she's your friend, that makes you a bit awesome, too."

"I'm not in third grade, Linus."

Linus laughed. "This is coming across all *Schoolhouse Rock*, isn't it?"

"A little."

"Adam." For the first time, Linus looked away, moving his hand and tapping his fingers in pretend interest on the side of Adam's lemonade. "You–" he looked up on "you" then looked away again– "are a big, beautiful guy. You give off this vibe of somebody trying to hide their wounds, wounds you didn't deserve but maybe you think you did." He looked up again. "I'll bet you didn't. I'll bet you money."

But Adam had started blushing furiously at "beautiful" and was only thinking of how he could keep Linus from noticing.

"I'm not swooping in on someone vulnerable," Linus said. "I want to be clear on that. That's not me." He shrugged. "But you've always seemed nice. Always seemed cute. And I just..." He tapped Adam's lemonade glass again, and Adam was surprised to hear Linus's voice do a little wobble. "I know what it's like. I know what all of it's like."

"Hello," Angela said, in a particular way, standing at the end of the table. "Hi, Linus." But she was looking squarely at Adam.

"Hey, Angela," Linus said, scooting back out.

"What are you doing?" Angela asked him.

He stopped, took a breath, looked at Adam. "Asking Adam out on a date. When he's ready. Or, you know, just to hang out."

With a little wave, he left them, not even sitting back at his own table. Turned out he'd been there waiting for his sister to finish a job interview to be a waitress. She got the job. Linus, eventually, got his date.

"My eyes are burning," Sarah says, and she means it literally. She gazes now upon the unfiltered glory of the Queen, something no one is meant to see, certainly none of Sarah's kind, not this close. She will be blind in moments if she does not look away.

For now, the faun does not care what happens to this clearly doomed mortal.

For here is his Queen, here she is.

"My Queen," he asks, "can you hear me?"

"Where am I?" she answers, and his heart rejoices. "What is this place?"

"You are trapped, my Queen. This spirit holds you here—"

"This spirit holds me here." She gazes still on Sarah, who is starting to whine at the pain. "This spirit holds me to this place, this body."

The Queen looks to the faun. Sarah gasps with relief. "How dare they?" says the Queen. "By what presumption do they—"

And she is suddenly gone again as she lets go of Sarah's hand.

For a moment there—

For a moment, she was herself again, but she cannot fully remember who that was or is. She is back in the company of this spirit, this one who has bound her.

This one who has come looking for her proper home.

In hopes that— thinks the Queen. In hopes that it will free her.

But is she the only one who needs freeing? And why this place? Why this person, rubbing her eyes and moaning on this foul-smelling couch in clothes that have gone too long without washing? What seemed so clear moments ago is now muddied.

"Why am I here?" she says aloud, and this person, this human, this Sarah, hears her.

"To punish me?" Sarah asks, fear covering her voice.

"It wasn't you who killed me," the Queen says.

"Oh, Katie." Sarah begins to cry, wincing at how the tears sting her injured eyes. "I should never have got you into this. It's my fault. It's my stupid fault."

"You were my home," the Queen says, remembering the fact of it, trying, struggling to remember the feeling that had been attached to it. "You were my best friend."

"You were *mine*, Katie," Sarah says, weeping now, then she says again, "I should never have got you into this."

The question rises in the Queen, in the spirit, twisting around the braid the two of them make together, this new third being their combination has created, the question rises and rises until it must be spoken, until it absolutely must—

"Are you to blame?" the Queen asks Sarah, and she genuinely doesn't know.

But she will kill whoever is there to take it.

Here. Now. Again. The whole reason for the two o'clock visit in the first place. Well, not the *whole* reason, but the opportunities and locations were still more infrequent than most people would think, so they took them when they found them.

And it was different with Linus in so many ways.

There were their respective heights, to start – it couldn't be ignored, so they didn't – but it was much more easily managed than Angela's questions would ever make it seem. "How do you keep from hitting your head? Doesn't he just *fall off* sometimes?"

"You went out with Chester Wallace," Adam would reply. "He's almost three feet taller than you."

"Yeah," Angela said, "but I just looked at it as a kind of obstacle course. You jump over some parts, you duck under others, then you climb the rope at the end and everyone gets a Diet Coke."

"What are you smiling at?" Linus whispered to him now, smiling a little himself.

"Nothing, just ... what a picture we must make."

"No pictures. Not ever."

"I don't *want* a picture–"

"Because those things never go away. We're going to have a president one day and she's going to be called Hayden and she's going to have a sun tattooed on the back of her neck and she would be the best president we've ever had ever except on day four of her term, someone finds those pictures she took after a peace rally with that nice beardy activist who said he didn't believe in mementos but that taking pictures 'got him in the mood' and he'd totally erase them later because he respected her too much."

And here was another difference. "How do you do that?"

"Do what?"

"Concentrate on two things at once."

Linus stretched forward awkwardly to kiss him on the lips. "I'm only concentrating on one thing, Adam."

Compared with Enzo, sex with Linus was a whole other world. Enzo wasn't a talker. Linus really, really was, and it turned out Adam quite liked it. The vibe was completely different, too. With Enzo, there were moments of what Adam could only describe as desperation. They *had* to do it, they *had* to get each other's clothes off, Enzo *had* to get inside Adam (the few times Adam had topped Enzo, there had been no *had to* about it, just lengthy negotiations and a process so clinical Adam hadn't even ended up enjoying it which, looking back, may have been Enzo's plan all along).

But with Linus, there was always a smile. Always. Like a kiss was something enjoyably secret. Like a hand on Adam's bottom was an almost old-fashioned advance (just like the word "bottom"). Like Linus was enlisting Adam in the funnest, funniest thing two people could do together.

It had never been funny with Enzo. Enzo was pushy, rough, assertive in a way that Adam (or Linus) never dared. He never would have stopped to ask if Adam was comfortable, never *did*, just assumed that Adam would get used to it, assumed Adam liked it that way. Sometimes Adam did. But sometimes it wasn't fun at all. Sometimes the pain never stopped and Adam would close his eyes, waiting for Enzo to finish, waiting for that grunt and gasp that Enzo always did, before he collapsed around Adam's neck, panting into his collarbone. Then he'd withdraw, two fingers holding the condom in place, which he then snapped off, threw into the bin by his bed and lay down to wait for Adam to finish himself.

Was that fair? Not Enzo's behaviour, but Adam's memory of it. Was it accurate? Was it hindsight rearranging things to make Adam more of the victim? He genuinely didn't know. But when he jerked off at home, he still hated himself for picturing Enzo more often than Linus.

"You're gone again," Linus whispered. "I need you here."

"Why are you whispering? We're alone in the house, aren't we?"

"Yeah, but…" Linus pushed gently but deeply. Adam breathed again. "Doesn't this feel like our own little world? Our own place, just the two of us, separate not only from other people, but from existence altogether?" He pushed again. "Like time has stopped. Like it's stopped and…"

"…and? God, that feels good."

"Yeah?"

"Yeah."

"Adam," Linus said, just Adam's name, putting his face into Adam's chest, nosing around the few blond hairs that sprouted there. He kissed the space between Adam's nipples, inhaling deeply, smelling Adam's skin. Most of Linus's upper body was between Adam's rucked-up thighs, Adam's ankles crossed against Linus's back. Adam lowered one foot until it came up against the ridge of Linus's butt, which – as previously mentioned – was a thing of almost punishing beauty. And something Linus shared much more democratically than Enzo ever had. Not that that was the one thing they always had to do. There were plenty of other things. Plenty. Linus was also a *lot* less single-minded in what he liked than Enzo ever was.

And Enzo definitely didn't have the butt of a dancer.

"You're so beautiful," Adam whispered, even quieter than Linus had. "You're so fucking beautiful, Linus." Linus kissed him again on the chest. Adam scooped up Linus's face in his hands. "No, I mean it." He ran his thumbs gently across Linus's cheeks, under the lower edge of his spectacles – which he amusingly kept on, both of them liking it, Linus in particular liking being able to see – and down around Linus's lips.

"Wish I was tall enough to kiss you properly like this," Linus said.

"What you're doing right now is pretty good on its own."

Taking the encouragement, Linus pushed again. And again. "Faster?" he asked.

Adam nodded. Yeah, faster was pretty good, all right.

And this, *this* was the rebuke to the Wades of the world, this was what Wade would never understand. Marty neither. Not even Enzo most of the time, now that Adam thought about it. There was so much more to it than just the body. The body was important, obviously, but in their different ways, neither Wade with his sleaze, nor Marty in his refusal to imagine beyond himself, nor Enzo in his just-friends retrospective boundary, none of them could see past the body. So many people couldn't when it wasn't society's usual combo.

But here, now, again, this was more than the body, or the mind, or the personality. It wasn't holy, that was a whole other mess, but it was something that could be touched only here. He'd touched it – to various degrees and from various angles – with Enzo a few times, with Philip Matheson, even with Larry from the teen choir. But nowhere like how he could touch it with Linus.

Then why–? Why why why–

Look at Linus, look at him there, look at the cute

whorl of hair where it parted on the crown of his head, look at the hand that ran across Adam's stomach, look at the skin at the bend of his elbow where the fold gave him a little tan line. Just look at him. Look at him loving Adam.

"I love you," Adam said. He said it to Linus.

Linus gave him a mischievous wink. "Doesn't count when you say it during sex." But then Linus noticed the tears squeezing out of Adam's eyes on either side and, with gentleness, brushed them away. "Adam?"

"Please don't leave me unloved," Adam answered, and cried some more, ashamed.

"The blame," the Queen says again. "I keep looking for it. Where is it? Where is the blame?"

The faun moves around her to try and calm this Sarah, who continues to weep, her fear obviously growing that this may not, after all, be a drug dream. He does this not out of compassion, for he can smell her weakness from here, but because this person has some hold, some claim on the spirit that traps his Queen. Strong enough to make it release her for a moment, and if he can make the release happen again–

"Where is the blame?" the Queen keeps asking.

Sarah stares back at the Queen, her red eyes wide, unburning as this spirit again masks the Queen's full glory.

At least he knows she is in there still. Strong and magnificent.

He will not miss his chance a second time.

• • •

"I find a strand of it in myself," the Queen hears herself say. "I do find it there."

But then she thinks, feels, reaches out, and knowing exactly what blame is – a human construct, one of its blackest and most selfish and self-blinding – she can find further strands of it, emanating in all directions, for blame is something that is shared but denied in equal measure.

"And yes," she says to Sarah, "I find a strand in you."

She sees that Sarah is afraid of this sentence, but welcomes it, too, a woman used to the burden of blame, secretly wanting it even if it kills her, because at least it is familiar.

"But so much less than what you think binds you," the Queen says. "The bigger strand is within me and yet again that is not even the biggest portion."

Like a cloud parting, Sarah finally seems to see, to really see.

"Is it…?" Sarah sits up, shock stilling her convulsions, stilling even the pain in her eyes, for she now looks at her friend, her friend who was murdered. "Is it really you?"

And she takes the Queen's hand.

The faun leaps.

"It's all right," Linus said, holding him a few minutes later, curved against him in the bed, breathing into the bend of his neck.

"I don't even know," Adam said. "I really don't."

"Wade, probably."

"God, don't say his name."

"Anything happening at home?"

"Marty got a girl pregnant."

Linus sat all the way up for that. "I beg your pardon? Why wasn't that the first thing you said when you walked in the door?"

"Wade, remember? And Angela."

"Well, as *remarkable* as the news that Marty's not a virgin actually is, that's not really enough to make you cry. Is it?"

"No."

"What's up then, babe?"

Adam wished he knew. Everything was always so

clear in books and movies. Everyone always knew their reasons. But real life was such a mess. Just look at today so far. The release with Linus was so wonderful – and though they were currently in an interruption, what they'd been leading to had pulled *so* strong on his heart – and yeah, the thing with Wade and Angela leaving and the tension at home and the still-pending afternoon at the church to help out his dad, and–

"It's Enzo, isn't it?" Linus said, just a little bit too quietly.

"No," Adam said, immediately. But then he wondered. Because underneath everything else, today was the day Enzo left forever.

"I don't mind," Linus said, sounding like he minded.

"You should mind. *I* mind."

Linus lowered his head until his chin rested on Adam's chest. "I wish I knew how he got a hook so deep in your heart. He's not even very nice."

"No," Adam said. "Well, he could be, but no. Not on the whole."

Linus tapped his middle finger over Adam's actual heart. "And yet he's still in there."

"It's not him, Linus, that's not why I'm crying."

"Maybe a little."

"Maybe a little. But if so, then only a little." He wondered if that were true. He hoped it was. And maybe it was.

"Then what is it?"

"Linus–"

"Is it me?"

"*No*–"

"I know he told you lies. Or things he believed were true when he said them but he let be untrue later. I haven't done that, Adam. And I'm not an angel here or anything, but I haven't lied to you. Not about us. Not about how I feel."

"I know–"

"Is it the height difference?"

"Jesus, no–"

"Is it because I'm more obviously gay than you, because sometimes there's internal homophobia–"

"It's *definitely* not that."

"So it *is* something?"

Adam suddenly felt like he was falling, like the centre of the bed beneath him had opened up and he had tumbled through, leaving Linus on the lip, looking down on him, too far to reach. All the time. He felt like this all the time. That everyone up there was out of reach. Linus, even Angela sometimes, definitely his family–

"Don't leave me unloved." Linus repeated his words. "What did you mean? It can't be that Enzo was the only one who loved you because–"

"That's not it. It *isn't*."

"Then what?"

Adam breathed now. There it sat. There it always sat, waiting to be said. "Oh, hell. I know what it is."

"What is it?"

"Why I haven't been letting myself love you back. Not properly."

Linus's forehead crimped at this, like he'd just taken a small blow.

"No," Adam said, "I don't mean it like that."

"Then how do you mean it?"

"Linus, I…"

"I can't love you any more than I do," Linus said, sadly. "I don't know how. I keep hoping it's enough. If it's not–"

"It is. It's me who's got the issue."

Linus started to pull away. "I knew it," he said. "I knew you couldn't let him go–"

"It's *really* not Enzo, Linus, I swear."

Linus was sitting up now, looking down at him, wounded. He waited, though.

"Today," Adam said, "this morning, Marty stopped me on my run to tell me about the girl he got pregnant and how they were going to get married and how her name meant happiness or something."

"This is the Russian girl?"

"Belarusian, and no, someone new."

"Go Marty."

"But he said… We were talking and he said…" Adam's throat tightened and he grimaced. "He said what I feel isn't real love. That I think it is, but it isn't. That I'm fooling myself because…"

Linus finished for him. "Because how could this ever be as real as the girl he got pregnant after meeting her five minutes ago."

Adam looked at Linus, almost desperately, his eyes

widening. "Oh, my God. Linus, I believed him. I *believed* him. I *still* believe him. There's still a voice in my head saying this isn't real, that it can't be."

"Because I'm not a girl?"

"That, and because…" He couldn't finish, his throat was too tight, his face screwed up, the tears coming painfully now, like a choke. Linus gently pulled himself closer again, onto Adam's chest, touching Adam's face lightly.

"Because," Linus said, finishing Adam's sentence again, "Adam Thorn doesn't deserve it. And never will."

"I'm sorry," Adam said.

"You are *so* not the one who should be sorry." Linus kissed Adam's nose, chin, lips. Adam just cried for a little while more, but then he began to kiss Linus back. And some more. He could taste himself in Linus's mouth, smell his own body on Linus's lips, knew Linus could do the same. The kisses grew deeper, hungrier. Adam could feel himself responding, could feel *Linus* responding.

But it was different from before. That was great fun, the usual smiles, the togetherness, but this was… This was intimacy.

He put his hands down Linus's body, pressed it into his own, smelled it, touched it, put his ear against Linus's chest to hear his heart, but always returning to the kiss, always, always. They didn't speak this time, but Linus was here, right now, in this space, with Adam, nosing his way into Adam's crevices, hands pulling him closer and closer, as if trying to merge them into one person, and with a gentle push, guiding himself back inside Adam, an act that didn't feel like penetration, but like *com*bination.

And here, now, again, was Linus. The low scars on his back where he'd had lung nodules removed when he was a child. The faint line of hair that extended down between his butt cheeks. The mole on the front of his right thigh. And the mid-sex scent of him, close and private, not sweat but something different, something only for Adam, as the point of no return was reached.

"I'm gonna come," Linus whispered, almost as a question, meeting Adam's eyes. Adam nodded. Linus stiffened – Adam could feel Linus's butt flex under the pad of his foot – held his breath for a second, then let it out in a gasp. They said nothing, but Linus's hand was already on Adam, helping him the rest of the way. It only took a moment, and when it was done, they were still there, panting together, the muscles of their bodies relaxing towards the next few seconds, but not just yet, not just yet.

"My Queen," says the faun, a forbidden, fatal arm around her, trying to pull her physically from the grip of this spirit. He can feel the separation, caused again by the touch of Sarah, who watches him goggle-eyed, though those same eyes burn again as the Queen separates from the spirit of the dead girl.

"You dare touch me!" thunders the Queen. "You dare–!"

And she stops. The faun stops, too, feeling an unexpected resistance. The Queen has paused.

The spirit – who is still the Queen, who is still the spirit, who is still the Queen – remains caught by the hand of Sarah, who for the moment has wisely abandoned all attempts at sense.

"Hold," says the Queen, softly, but unmistakably a command. The faun pauses. She is half in and half out of the spirit, as if she has leaned back and merely found the spirit sitting in front of her. "Hold," the Queen says again.

And they both listen.

"You have to release me," says the spirit.

"You have to release me," says the Queen in perfect tandem, watching like one of her great hunting pikes who wait patiently to strike.

"To whom are you speaking, my Queen?" the faun asks.

"Katie?" says Sarah. "I've missed you so much. I can't… I can't even seem to get through the days any more."

"You have to let me go," says the spirit, says the Queen.

Sarah looks down at the hand that holds the girl's arm.

"I do not mean your hand," says the spirit, says the Queen.

"My Queen," the faun says. "There is doom coming if you do not–"

"I said, Hold," says the Queen, not looking at the faun.

"You must release me or you will never be released," says the spirit, says the Queen to Sarah. "You must let me go. You are not to blame."

Sarah begins to weep, her hand still on the Queen.

"You must let go now, my Queen," says the faun.

"There is nothing a Queen must do," says the Queen, eyes still on the spirit and the girl on the couch.

"You lose yourself within her. The spirit will drag you to your death. To the death of us all."

"The spirit hunts. The spirit quests for her own release." The Queen raises the smallest of fingers, but it is enough for the faun to let her go immediately. She sinks back into the spirit, but before she does, she tells him, "I will follow her. I will go where she leads."

"It may cost you, my Queen. It may cost you dear."

"All the best journeys do, faun."

Then she is gone, gripped again by the spirit, now freed from Sarah, who she leaves weeping on the sofa. She stands, no longer seeing the faun, perhaps no longer even knowing he is there, and she heads to the front door, to who knows what beyond.

And once again, there is nothing the faun can do but clear the memories of Sarah and follow his Queen, glancing at the sun and wondering at his last day in existence.

"Off to the church now?" Linus said, leaning in Adam's driver side window.

"Yeah," Adam said. "Setting up for tomorrow's services. His main ushers are both out sick, and I'm always backup number one."

Linus leaned further inside. "You still smell like us."

"My dad won't know what that is." Adam looked up. "Will he?"

"You can shower. Again."

"I'm late as it is."

"I'll see you at Enzo's party, yeah?"

"You're still going? After..."

"I get to see you and there's free beer. Of course I'm still going." Linus kissed him again. "I wasn't kidding. I know it's high school. I know we're young. I know these things may or may not last or even if they should. But I love you, Adam Thorn. Today, right now, I do."

"And I love you," Adam said, seriously, meaning it.

"Maybe not yet," Linus grinned, "but possibly soon."

Adam drove off, waving in the rear-view mirror to Linus who, right now, yes, he did love. Enough to make his heart ache. He hoped it would last.

He hoped he would deserve it.

He glanced at his phone as he turned onto the main road into town. A missed call from Marty. None from his parents. Nothing from Angela, but she'd probably just got stuck at work. One from Karen at the Evil International Mega-Conglomerate asking if he was okay. And–

You're a good person, Adam. Don't ever let them tell you you're not.

From Linus.

He set his phone back down and drove on, not noticing until he parked at the church that the red rose he'd meant to give Linus was still sitting on the passenger seat.

6

THE HOUSE UPON THE ROCK

"That's going to be too far apart," Big Brian Thorn said. "We've got fifteen rows to fit in here."

"As a tall person, I can swear truthfully that these aren't too far apart."

"You won't be sitting here. You're always up in the balcony. Don't think I haven't noticed."

"I'm not the tallest person in the entire congregation."

"On average, you're well above. Fifteen rows."

The overflow room was on the left of the sanctuary. It was also the church's main activity area and was used all week for a nursery in the mornings and AA meetings in the evenings, both bringing in rent that The House Upon The Rock didn't like to admit it needed. Saturdays were for an early morning Men's Bible Study that to Adam's relief he was still technically too young to be forced to go to. Today, that had been followed by the teen choir practising the musical they were going to inflict on the church on Labor Day – Adam's tunelessness being so pronounced even his dad didn't encourage him to sing – followed by what was supposed to be his dad's two main ushers helping him set up the space for services tomorrow. But one was having thyroid surgery and the other had fallen down a flight of stairs, probably (but not provably) drunk. So it was down to Adam to help his dad make the church ready. Fifteen rows of five long padded benches apiece to make up an overflow room that would, at best, end up a third full.

"Why isn't Marty helping?" Adam asked, hoisting his sixtieth bench into place.

"I don't want to talk about Marty right now," his dad said, not looking his way.

"But helping here could be penance."

He got a glance for that. "We're not Catholics, Adam. We don't do penance. We do forgiveness."

"If you've forgiven him, then he should *definitely* be here helping."

"I haven't forgiven him." Big Brian Thorn stopped where he was bringing in the cart full of hymnals that Adam would soon be setting out on the benches. "God help me, I haven't forgiven him yet."

Adam couldn't remember the last time that look on his father's face had been caused by his brother and not by Adam straying from a path so narrow it was a wonder *any* Christian here could see it. The novelty was so great, he even found himself asking, "Do you want to talk about it?"

"I do not," Big Brian Thorn said, getting back to work. The overflow room was only the start. The cameras that broadcast the sermon to the web needed to be checked, the sound system tested – the teen choir had a history of not putting it back the way they found it – and, as it was that time of the quarter, the Jacuzzi behind the cross at the front of the sanctuary needed to be cleaned, filled and warmed for the baptisms taking place tomorrow. This would be Adam's job, the last he needed to finish before he was free to help Angela with the pizzas for the "get-together".

They worked mostly in silence, for which Adam was grateful. He was even more grateful his dad trusted him to do it (mostly) and kept a good distance. Adam really didn't know how strong the smell of Linus might be.

"How long have you known?" his dad said, looking at two hymnals he was holding but not putting anywhere.

Adam's stomach fell. "Known what?"

"About your brother."

Adam swallowed in relief. "This morning. He caught me at the end of my run."

"Why you first?"

Adam was about to answer, but realized his dad was asking himself, not actually interested in Adam's take. Adam answered anyway. "Probably just a warm-up. See how the words sounded when he said them out loud. See if they'd kill him or if they were just words."

"They were more than just words."

"There are positives," Adam said. "You'll be a grand-father."

"I'm forty-five. My hair isn't even grey."

"It will be if Marty keeps the surprises coming."

His dad set down the hymnals. "Don't be glib. The young are always glib. And look what happens." He turned and left, heading back, Adam assumed, to his office. There was a sermon to write, after all. Adam wondered what topics it could possibly be covering.

The Queen and the spirit who binds her wish to enter a prison.

This is going to cause issues the faun doesn't know if he can properly address. Breaking down the doors and walls will, of course, be no problem; his strength is that of any hundred of these fragile creatures with their busy, fuddled lives. But that would attract more attention. He would be seen by too many eyes, more than he could hope to control, and for a creature who depended on myth, too much fact could prove quite fatal.

But the Queen is determined. There she goes, approaching the prison up a curved, fenced road intended only for the cars that guard it. It will be mere moments before one passes this way.

"My lady, please," he says, though he doesn't know how much she hears now. He is watching the sun as it leans down its arc. It is a summer day, which is a fortune, but the afternoon will not last forever. There will be dusk. Then that

same sun will set, spelling a doom the only comfort of which is that, if it comes, he will be gone before its full manifest.

The inevitable police car pulls down around the curve, close enough so the faun can see the astonishment of the man behind the wheel as he comes upon first a dead woman in a drowned dress, then a seven-foot faun following at a respectful distance.

It begins, thinks the faun, and he moves forward to start the long battle his Queen requires him to wage.

The sheer, solid fact of the car is a surprise to her, though it shouldn't be. It stops short, its brakes squealing as it rocks forward. The door opens. The man's hand is already on his gun, his face a picture of confusion.

Hostile confusion.

"Are you all right, ma'am?" he asks, in a tone convinced that no, she isn't and no, he might not be either.

But then...

An astonished recognition. For them both.

"Oh, it is fate," she says. "It is fate that has brought this."

"I know you," the man says, hand still on his gun. "But you must be her sister."

"You found me," says the Queen. "In the lake, you found me."

"You don't belong on this road," he answers. "Neither of you, and sir, I'm placing you under arrest immediately for indecent exposure–"

"'Sir'?" she says, but the policeman is suddenly on his back, his eyes unseeing, laid out almost delicately next to his still-running car. She moves to him, hovers over him, not understanding what's happened.

"You found me," she tells him, needs to tell him. "You pulled me from the shallows. You tried to revive me hours after anything would have helped. I felt your hands on my chest. The muscle of my heart contracted under your weight." She leans down to the man's face, her dead hands touching his temples. "You arrested my killer. You put him here." She looks up the road. The prison can't be seen, but it's just beyond the rise. "This was meant to be. There are greater powers at work."

She rises. She leaves the man behind, more certain than ever of where she's going.

The faun removes the man's memories of the Queen, having laid him on the ground. He knows bullets will not work on him, but in her current shape, he cannot be sure of the same for the Queen.

There is no time to move the car or the man. They will have to remain and cause further chaos, further trouble.

"There are greater powers at work," the Queen says.

He wonders, as he hurries after her, does she mean herself? Or him? Or is something else, something terrible pushing them relentlessly on?

Adam had been an unquestioning churchgoer for most of his life, until all of a sudden he wasn't. And then he was again. And then not. And then again, when he deleted all his porn and questionable apps in a righteous frenzy after rededicating his life to Jesus in a handwritten letter to his parents, saying he was frightened at how the world was heading, that the Antichrist must surely come soon, and that he was pledging himself to God and to the church. There had been tears from everyone.

He was thirteen, and by the next day, he was sorely regretting both letter and deletions. He'd been trying to regain the cache of porn ever since, and every time he acted up too badly, his mother or father would produce the letter and ask where this tender-hearted Adam had gone.

"The Prodigal Son was the most beloved," they said, more than once.

Where does that leave Marty? he never asked.

The blind faith boomerang had stopped with Enzo.

"What do you do with that?" he'd asked Angela. "Here's this thing, this love, that should be *proof* of God, and they're telling you it's the opposite."

"I've never understood your parents," she said.

"I guess I really haven't either."

"My church isn't anything like that. We just had a wedding for probably the two oldest lesbians in the state. Can you imagine being in your eighties and still wanting to try something new?"

"That story is why I'm not allowed to come with you on Sundays."

She shrugged. "We don't go that often anyway. And even then, it's only so Mom can see friends."

"I used to think this was how everyone's life was. That everyone sat around the dinner table talking about the End Times."

"We do. We just mean another Republican presidency."

He smiled to himself in the sound booth at the church, resetting the levels where, yep, the teen choir had ludicrously amped up the bass *and* the treble, leaving the middle feeds all but silent. If Big Brian Thorn – a *basso profundo* by temperament and training – tried bellowing into a microphone set to that, he'd both shatter glass and be completely incomprehensible.

Adam took out his phone. *Dad's actually not being too insane about Marty. Hurt, but not insane.*

Not yet anyway, Angela texted back. *How was Linus? None of your business.*

Did you sex him?

None of your business.

Did you sex him up real good?

NOYB. I've still got a couple hours here. Pizza place at 7?

I'll be here.

For now.

Don't start.

He paused, then he typed, *I love you more than probably any other person on this planet. Including myself.*

She texted a tearful emoji and *Don't make me cry at work!*

"Are you done in here?" frowned his dad, leaning into the tiny sound room. It had literally been converted from a bathroom beside the balcony sometime before Adam was born. It could only fit one person at a time, and even then, Adam's elbows bumped either wall.

"Almost," Adam said.

"You'd be past almost if you weren't wasting time on the phone."

"I'm meeting Angela after this. I was arranging it."

His dad softened. Even in his worst moods, Angela's racial difference gave him a chance to feel magnanimous. Big Brian Thorn liked to feel magnanimous. "She's welcome to come to the Labor Day musical, you know. She's always welcome here."

"Yeah, but do you know what pizza places are like on Labor Day? Everyone in the world is having one last summer party. It's basically their Black Friday."

To Adam's surprise, Brian Thorn almost smiled.

"I saw the craziest thing today," his dad said. "Driving here."

"What's that?"

"A man dressed up as a goat."

"Beg pardon?"

"I know, that's what I thought. Proper costume, too, movie quality. Not just something you'd slip on but like someone had glued actual hair all over him."

"What kind of costume is a *goat*?"

"Well, he was standing up, I guess. Not a goat on all fours."

"So ... a faun? Or, what do you call them? A satyr?"

His dad frowned, obviously disliking the move from animal into pagan. "Maybe they're filming something around here. Some HBO thing."

"The Satyr Housewives of Frome, Washington."

"I don't even begin to understand that joke."

"At least you understood it was a joke. That's a start."

His dad almost smiled again. Maybe, Adam thought, as Big Brian Thorn left for the lower level to test the microphones, maybe this is what Marty felt like all the time. Marty had gone unexpectedly Prodigal, which left Adam the son closer to home, the one to be allied with, the one not quite so lost, free, for a moment, from the Yoke.

Interesting, Adam thought.

The shouting begins before they even fully crest the hill.

"Get down!"

"Hands where I can see them!"

"What the hell is that?"

"I said, GET DOWN!"

The faun raises his hands – an accidental show of surrender that probably stops them from firing – and all three guards fall to the ground, unconscious. His only recourse is to remove this entire day from their memories. A blunt solution, but the only one available in the time they have left.

The Queen stops at what seems to be the entrance, a surprisingly unobtrusive one for a building so secure. She reaches for the handle, but he knows, of course, that it will not simply open, it is a prison. He moves to help her–

The door flies off its hinges, the metal of it warping as if punched by a giant hand. The faun has to step out of the *way as it clangs down the drive, probably bouncing all the way to the car they stopped on the way up.*

"My lady?" says the faun.

The door comes open in her hand, more than open, she merely has to brush it with the intention of it not being there and it is destroyed, flung from her sight.

It is unexpected and yet feels right. I have power, she thinks, power older than civilization. She tests it again, waving her fingers at the woman who approaches holding a gun. The woman drops to the floor, a threat no longer.

I lit a fire with my hands, she thinks. I moved through the air by thought alone.

She remembers these things. And has always known them.

I am two. I am the spirit and the second spirit that binds me. We are growing closer. We are blurring into one.

"You are the Queen," says a voice behind her.

She does not look back, merely answers, "Yes, I am the Queen," and tears another door from its hinges.

No one looked at the Jacuzzi between the baptisms, and even with the cushioned lid on top, there was always a layer of dust inside as well as – this time – one, two, three dead mice that Adam picked out with rubber gloves. Once, in a mystery still unsolved, he'd found an open box for a diaphragm, but try as he might, there wasn't a single person in the church he could imagine having left it there.

He'd been baptized himself at eight years old in this very spot. Big Brian Thorn scoffed at the notion that full-body immersion was going out of fashion – it was, but scoffing brought in the people who still wanted it – and had baptized Adam himself, praying over him, asking him the questions ("Do you dedicate your life to Jesus Christ as your Personal Lord and Saviour?" "I do"), and had dunked him. He had been so small that the congregation couldn't actually see him, and – once dunked – his dad had lifted him entirely out of the water, over the lip of the doors behind the choir and said, "Can you all see my boy?"

The congregation had laughed, heartily.

"Not at *you*," his mother had said at his bedside that night.

"Yes, they were," Adam sniffled.

"Honestly, Adam, do you really think the world revolves around you? Do you think all those people, friends of your father, would sit there in a worshipful place and laugh at *you*?"

Adam knew the answer was supposed to be no, so he only said "yes" in his head.

For a moment, as he scrubbed the dust that had been baked in by a surprisingly hot summer, he wondered how his parents saw him, what he seemed like to them on a day-to-day basis. Up until today, Marty had been such a perfect son – blond, well-behaved, boring, yes, but safely so – what must they have thought when Adam came along? He, too, was blond, and well-behaved for that matter, never in trouble at school, no run-ins with the police, hardly ever even tardy.

"But there's something different about the boy," he'd overheard his father say, a few years before even the baptism. He'd been eavesdropping from upstairs, his bedhead hair sticking through the railings, thrilled and a little sick at the risk of being out of bed, listening to his parents' secret conversations.

"He's too little to say that about, isn't he?" his mother had answered. They were sitting in front of the fireplace, his mom with a Christian romance novel, his dad with one, too, a secret vice neither of them would admit. But the way his mom had answered left the question open, not as if she was disagreeing, but as if she was curious at how his dad might convince her.

"He's ... *dreamy*," his dad said. "Off in his own little world."

"You do that. You disappear."

"You know what I mean, Lydia. His eyes are so smart. Like there's all these little calculations going on in there that you'll never know about."

Adam liked the sound of this.

"Like he's judging you," his mother said.

Adam liked the sound of this less, because though he didn't understand what she meant exactly, her tone clearly suggested it wasn't anything desirable.

"I don't say 'judging'," his father said. "I wouldn't say that. He's obviously bright, and that should be encouraged. It's more ... you watch him at the church and he's looking at the other little ones and you can see him, wondering."

"Wondering what?"

"Exactly. Wondering what to do. Wondering how to talk to them. Wondering how soon he can leave and go back to talking to adults."

"Ooh, yeah, he does do the adult-talking thing. I caught Dawn Strondheim telling him about her divorce."

"That woman."

"I know. Though, knowing him, he probably gave her advice."

"I'm not saying it's a bad thing necessarily. Maybe that's God's gift to him. The noticing. The wisdom beyond his years."

"Are you comparing him to Jesus? Because that's taking it a little far."

Adam, who liked being compared to Jesus, wasn't happy about this part either.

"It just bothers me sometimes," his father said. "Are we that much of a mystery to him that he needs to spend all that time figuring us out? What goes on in that little head?"

"God in his endless variety, sweetheart. Be a boring life if they *weren't* different. Marty is a good, good boy. I wish Adam were a little less of a suck-up, but he's a good boy, too."

"I think we're getting near for done," his dad said, coming in now, catching him in the same half-dream state they'd been talking about that very night.

"I've still got to fill the Jacuzzi up," Adam said. "Get the water heating."

"Yeah, but–" his dad looked at his watch, being of an age where he still went there first rather than his phone– "not bad. You did good work today."

Adam turned on the water. It'd be a good twenty minutes filling, then he'd need to chlorinate and set it heating, but his dad was right: they'd done pretty well.

"Thanks. Plenty of time to get to Angela."

Big Brian Thorn sat down on the bench they used for those waiting to be baptized. This wasn't even a proper room, really, just a storage area his dad had turned into the baptismal, complete with benches and doors leading to where the choir robes were kept and where those getting baptized changed into baptismal garments. "You really care for her, don't you?"

"She's my best friend," Adam answered, simply. He'd decided not to tell his dad about Angela leaving yet. That felt like too personal a pain to be shared with someone as far away from him as his father.

"Not too many boys have a girl as a best friend," his father ventured, but Adam didn't think it was a poke. Oddly, it actually seemed like his father was genuinely making conversation.

"It's different now than when you were young," Adam said. "Fewer divisions."

"That's certainly true." His father leaned back on the bench, crossing his arms, looking down at his feet. "We thought you'd marry her, you know?"

Adam decided to ignore the past tense. "I don't think I'm her type. Too tall."

"Oh, people get over bigger things. You'd be surprised."

"Things like what?"

"Things like … things. It's amazing what you can do with the Grace of the Lord."

"Dad—"

"I'm not digging at you." He was still looking at his shoes. He sighed. "This thing with Martin has … thrown me."

Adam looked at him warily, trailing forgotten fingers in the water of the Jacuzzi. "It would throw anybody."

"Yes, I suppose it would." He looked up. He was grinning. It was strange. "I gotta tell you, Adam, and I don't mean this in a bad way, but you're the one we thought we'd never be surprised by. You'd think it would be Martin because he's ... Martin. Dependable, I'll-give-it-a-try Martin, but you... I don't think we'd be surprised by anything you did."

"That doesn't really sound like you don't mean it in a bad way."

"Adam–"

"So you wouldn't be surprised if I robbed a bank? Or murdered a small town?"

"Or won a Nobel Prize," his dad said. "Or saved a family from a burning house. I'm just saying... We're predictable people, Adam. It's what we depend on Christ for. It's what He promised us, that no matter what this life is like, there's something guaranteed to be waiting for us if we love Him and do His will. It's the great prediction." His father clasped his hands now, almost as he would during prayer. "But I think... I wonder if we take that too far into our lives. And put too much value on the predictable. And never find the value in the *un*predictable."

"Like me."

His dad's grin tightened. "I'm not getting at ya, Adam," he said again. "I'm trying to tell ya..."

He trailed off. Adam attempted to break the little weird tension that had arisen. "Your voice has gone folksy. Remember, I *know* you're not from Kentucky."

But his dad didn't so much as crack a smile. "I just wish…"

"What?" Adam asked, still idly trailing his fingers in the water, though his stomach was starting to knot.

His dad looked at him. "I wish we could be honest with each other. I wish that for all of us. I wish it for your mother. I wish it for Martin. And I wish it for you, son. I wish it for you and me. I wish you felt you could be completely honest with me. It hurts my heart that you're afraid."

For a moment, a long one, they just stared at each other, the rushing water the only sound. Adam thought each of them was hoping the other would break the silence first.

Once, at thirteen, Adam had perfectly innocently been kicked out of a friend's house in the middle of the night by the drunk boyfriend of the friend's mother asserting his authority during a sleepover. Adam had been thrown onto the street, barely even able to make a phone call to his dad. "Can you come?" was all he'd said.

Big Brian Thorn arrived with his sleeves pushed up, his eyes wide open, and an air of threat and menace that Adam would have felt terrified of if he hadn't been absolutely sure it wasn't for him. "Did he hurt you?" his dad had asked.

"No, I just want to go."

"Are you sure?"

"Yes, I'm sure."

They'd driven away, his dad even letting Adam cry from the shock of it all, rather than trying to get him to stop like he usually did. If the drunk boyfriend had laid a finger on him, Adam was fairly certain his dad might have beaten him all the way to death. If protectiveness was love, his dad was an avalanche of it.

But.

And it was a big "but", wasn't it?

The sermons, the fear and suspicion of Enzo (who, to be fair, they were right to be suspicious of), Marty telling him how much they all talked about him...

What was his father asking him here? What was his father *telling* him?

If it *could* be like this. If they *could* be honest with each other. If Adam didn't *have* to be afraid.

But he did, he did, he did.

Didn't he?

Big Brian Thorn was overbearing, punitive, capricious, not a big fan of the gays or anything alternative, but he clearly loved his sons, in his own flawed way. And if Adam would argue to himself that it wasn't love if it altered when it alteration found, it was a kind of love. Fierce, ferocious, baffled. He'd be lying if he said he looked at what Martin – up until this morning, at least – had always had with his parents and was never jealous.

He found it coming out of his mouth before he even knew what he was saying. "Something happened at work today, Dad."

There are ancient agreements with this world, agreements made before memory with the people who were first in this place, people who gave the faun and his Queen different shapes in their dreams and prayers, shapes that changed as the people did, shapes that become ever more elastic until he often doesn't know what physical form he will take when he steps out of the lake until he has done so. Still, as changeable as both sides were, they had once agreed to put a war to its end.

He, for example, has not wilfully eaten the flesh of one of these creatures for millennia. The impulse to hunt him in return was removed from their thinking. Reciprocity.

All of which will vanish if the Queen dies. She is the keystone between the worlds. Should she die, the treaty will be only the first thing to unravel. The universe will soon follow.

And so he catches the bodies before she can hit them with her full force, he drags them out of her way when they try to stop her; he replaces the throat of a man who tries to physically restrain her. The man is breathing as the faun leaves him behind, and for now that's the best he can manage.

She will not answer his questions, though he believes she can now hear him.

"My Queen," he says, reattaching an arm to a thankfully unconscious guardswoman, erasing the memory and the pain from her thoughts. "We must get you to safety. We must get you to the lake."

But she carries on, remorseless, relentless. He hasn't seen her like this since before the world began, when it needed forming, when she had to beat back the very darkness itself that threatened to consume them all.

The world is at stake again. He wonders if she will win this time. And if she doesn't, will he have time to eat anyone before the worlds disintegrate?

The man she seeks is deep within this prison. She can feel him there.

What does she want with him? She is unsure and she senses this confusion seeping through the identity that binds her. But the drive is not confused. The drive is pure. The drive is a torrent and she can only be swept along.

She destroys another iron door. Beyond is a corridor, barred rooms on either side. The bars are too close-set for the faces to peer at her from all but the most oblique angles, but she senses enormous curiosity here, a willingness to shout, a wish to leer and call—

But there is only silence as she steps in. The men – they are all men – stand as if they have taken a breath and held it. They do not shrink back, they are clearly men long past being afraid of anything, no matter how majestic, no matter how powerful, men who would take a moment to chew first if their own God asked them to rise from their dinner table.

But nor do they offer disrespect. The first two men, right and left, stare at her firmly, unwaveringly, and within them she recognizes the spark that drives some of these creatures. The one that compels them to consume too much, gorge themselves to the point of actual physical harm and beyond, the greed and gluttony that would burst their very skin if they could manage it. There is injustice here, certainly there is, there has never been a creature as unjust as these, but there is badness here, too, true and deep, eyes that lead down wells with no bottom.

"Judge me," the one to her right says.

"Judge me," echoes the one to her left.

"My Queen," she hears behind her, but she raises her hand to silence it.

"I will," she says. "I will judge you."

"He did what?" Big Brian Thorn said.

"He didn't come right out and say it," Adam said. "But it was all there."

"You're sure?"

"I'm sure."

"You're *sure*?"

"Well, no, I mean, like I said, he didn't come right out and say it but–"

"This man made a sexual advance on you?"

"That's what it felt like."

His dad flexed his fists for a moment, breathing heavily through his nose. "God forgive me if I say that what I'm feeling right now is that I'd like to kill him."

"The thought had occurred to me, too."

"And you're *sure*?"

"How many times are you going to ask?" The Jacuzzi was full now. Adam turned off the faucet and started flipping the heater switches.

"There's no way you could be misinterpreting him?"

"That's what *he* said."

"But surely he could have meant–"

"I saw the hard-on in his pants, Dad!"

Big Brian Thorn winced. There was so much in the sentence that would have been difficult for him to hear, his son saying "hard-on" pretty high among them.

Adam kept talking, was annoyed to find his voice shaking a little as he remembered, kept talking anyway. "He was ... touching me. He had his hands on my thighs. Pressing just a little too hard."

His dad looked up. "Pressing any way at all is too much."

"He was just... Testing the boundaries, I think. Seeing how much he could get away with."

"Sounds like you let him get away with a lot."

Adam's stomach went cold. "He shouldn't have touched me, Dad."

"No," his dad said, quickly. "No, of course not. He's in the position of power here. There's an abuse of authority."

Adam finished with the Jacuzzi. It would be ready for tomorrow morning's immersions, ready to cleanse the souls of the white-shirted believers who would let themselves be dunked by the massive man sitting a few feet away. The massive man who even his son could see was clearly wrestling with what to say.

Adam felt one of his infrequent-lately waves of affection for him. His dad's size – an enormous middle-aged belly now augmenting all that defensive lineman bulk

– his serious beard, his blue, blue eyes that only Marty had inherited. A man who felt he should get what he wanted but who kept finding himself falling just short. The news from Marty was an obvious blow, and now here was his somehow troubling second son adding the picture of a man wanting sex. Worse, *Wade* wanting sex.

Maybe it was as simple as that here was a confused man struggling to figure out how best to love him.

"Dad–"

"And you're sure you didn't lead him on?"

That man vanished in an instant. "What?"

His dad rubbed his nose distractedly but then got a look like he had cast the die, so why not follow it through? "Adam, we … *know*. Your mom and I. We know."

Adam ignored how his heart was racing. "Know what?"

"Don't play stupid. You had pornography on your laptop. *That* kind of pornography."

Adam didn't know where to go with this so decided to aim for invasion of privacy, which was always as good as an admission of guilt. "You looked on my *laptop*?"

"And we know you had an … *infatuation* with that Mexican boy–"

"He's Spanish."

"But that seemed to have passed and your mom found the pictures a while ago–"

"*Mom* found it?"

"You seemed to be doing so well. So … you know, close to Angela and…"

"And what?"

His dad looked him straight in the eye. "Do you know how much we pray for you? Pray for your healing?"

"I don't need healing."

"We all need healing."

"I don't need *that* kind of healing. Nobody does. Seriously, Dad, do you know what *year* it is?"

"I don't need to move with the times if the times are wrong–"

"And what are you saying anyway? That I led Wade *on*?"

Big Brian Thorn looked distinctly uncomfortable now. "I know the hormones of teenage boys. It can happen to anyone. Look at Martin."

"Marty is no longer a teenager."

"I'm just saying that, you know, if you … had a little *crush* on this manager–"

"*Wade?!*"

"Then maybe he thought you were … making yourself available."

Adam blinked at his father. Just blinked. They were in unknown territory here, in so many ways. This was, remarkably, the first time since the Wendy's that either of his parents had directly addressed the topic with him, though clearly they'd been doing so regularly with Marty. And if they'd found stuff on his laptop – nothing creepy, just the regular-looking kind of guy that Adam found himself preferring to professional porn – and not even *mentioned* it–

How dangerous did they think he was?

"Making myself available?" he said, feeling the fury rise. "What the fuck is that supposed to mean?"

His dad looked up sharply, angrily. "Do *not* use language like that in God's House."

"But it's okay to accuse your son of leading his manager into sexual harassment bordering on outright assault?"

"I'm just saying, maybe unconsciously–"

"I'm *seventeen*. He's my gross boss with a gross moustache and looks like a road so well travelled I need to wash my hands after just being near him."

"You let him put his hands on your thighs."

This landed like a slap. The words of blame he had put on his own self, now coming out of the mouth of his father.

"So I was asking for it," Adam said, his mouth dry. "Is that what you're saying?"

All Big Brian Thorn did in answer to his son was shrug. But there was fear in his eyes. Fear even Adam could see. He'd thought the word "dangerous" just now.

Well, if that's what they wanted.

"Do you know where I was this afternoon?" Adam said. "After leading my completely innocent boss into firing me unless I had sex with him?"

"Adam–"

"I was getting comfort in the bed of my boyfriend."

It was Big Brian Thorn's turn to look slapped. But not surprised. Not in the least surprised.

"Adam, I don't want to hear this."

"Yeah, well, I've heard a *lot* of things today I didn't want to hear, so I'm going to keep talking."

"No, you're not. And don't think you're going out tonight either."

"To the going-away party for Enzo? The boy I spent large portions of the last two years screwing?"

"*Adam–*"

"Which is actually not the right way around–"

"You will not speak to me this way! Not here–"

"But that's okay, because I like being on the bottom. That's what I did today with Linus."

"With ... what? Who?"

"Remember the boy you preached about? I mean, it's less of a surprise when you think about it. This is hardly a very big town–"

"You're seeing that ... *boy*?"

"More than seeing. There's quite a lot of sex involved."

"Stop this!"

Adam held out his wrists. "You can still smell him on me. That's why I've tried to keep my distance from you all afternoon. I didn't have a chance to wash him off my body."

His dad closed his eyes and started to pray, loudly. "Oh, Lord, please help my son. Please help him on his misguided path–"

"Then we did it a second time. Even better than the first, because it was like this new kind of closeness–"

"I rebuke this sin in the name of our Lord Jesus Christ–"

But Adam didn't *feel* rebuked. He felt powerful. He felt the thrill of burning down his own house. It wouldn't last, he knew that even then, but the moment had come for him to be dangerous, and finally, this once, he was going to take it.

"I had him inside me, Dad, so you can't even pretend it's a phase."

"I pray for you to cast the devil from this place–"

"Quite a lot of things with our mouths, too."

"Jesus, please, I beseech you–"

"He's really hairy down there, which you wouldn't think on such a clean-shaven guy–"

"ADAM!" his father shouted, in a voice Adam could remember him using only once or twice in his life. He tensed, realizing he was waiting to be struck. His father had risen, his arms were out from his bullish body, one meaty hand braced for a slap at the very least–

But it never came. Adam would forever wonder how much fight had gone on inside Big Brian Thorn not to land it.

"You will never speak to me like that again," his dad said to him.

"You're the one who begged me to be honest with you. Not my fault if you can't take it."

"You're going home. You're going straight home and you're not leaving the house for anything except church and whatever Christian school we're going to find for you."

"It's my senior year. I'm not changing schools."

"I'm not interested in your opinion on the matter."

"And I'm not interested in *yours*."

"Adam," his dad said, all warning now.

"*And* I'm going from here to meet Angela. *And* I'm going to the party with her. *And* I'm not going to stop seeing my boyfriend."

"Yes, you are."

And here, Adam did something he couldn't ever remember doing. He stepped towards his father, as a physical challenge, a show of the bravery his anger was making him feel but which he knew would run out fast.

His father, astonished, stepped back.

"Do you know *why* I'm going to do all those things?" Adam said. "Because they're my family. They love me. *They* are who I go to when things are hard. That hasn't been you for years, Dad, and do you really never wonder whose fault that is?"

"I am your father—"

"A father with conditions. I have to be a certain way to be your son."

"Through prayer, everything is possible—"

"I don't know, I've prayed for years to change your heart. Nothing's happened so far."

"Adam—"

"I'm going."

"You are not."

Adam waited to see if his dad would stop him. There was no contest if it came to bodily restraint. Adam had edged up taller, but his dad outweighed him by at least a hundred pounds.

But his dad didn't move.

"Do you even love me?" Adam asked.

"More than my own life," his dad said, immediately.

"But you don't want to have to *do* anything with that love. You don't want it to have to work."

"You have no idea how much I work to love you."

And there it was, the blow after all. Even Big Brian Thorn seemed to realize it because he didn't try to stop Adam as he left The House Upon The Rock, got into his car and drove off to find Angela.

Drove off to find his family.

She has killed them all, and they have welcomed it. They have seen the Queen that the faun sees, and she has judged them and found them wanting, a sentence they have accepted with a relief so palpable he could almost see it being expelled in the air.

One by one, they drop to the floor of their cells as she passes. He hurries to restore life to them, knowing even as he brings them back to simple unconsciousness that they will curse him in dreams for their revivification.

This is what the Queen does. This is why she must remain away, hidden from those who cannot see her truly. This is why the agreements were made in the first place. But they will fail if he cannot get her out of here.

It will not matter to him. He will be the first that she kills. But he values his world, values his own life, values his Queen's above all else. They will not end if he can help it.

And so he brings breath back into the lungs of the

dead men, one by one, as she kills them, one by one, steadily making her way to the end of the corridor.

The man she wants is in the last cell.

They are nearing an ending, the faun knows. He wishes he knew what it will be.

She reaches the man's cell. She turns to him. The Queen and the girl, Katie, turn to him, and they are now so interleaved that neither is entirely sure which of them speaks.

"Hello, Tony," they say. "My murderer."

7

THE GET-TOGETHER

"Oh, Adam," Angela said, as she set the last of tonight's pizzas on the conveyor belt that would take them under the flames.

"I know."

"Jesus."

"I *know*."

"Do you think they'll come here? It's not like they don't know where I work. Emery does all those big orders for your church teen group."

Adam's phone was a billboard of unanswered texts, most of which were variations on *Come home right now*. But they were only texts. No one had actually called him. Except, oddly, Marty. Over and over again from Marty. Who finally texted, too. *Please tell me you're okay, bro*.

"I think they're waiting for me," he said. "I've got to choose to come home. That's what the Prodigal Son always does."

"It's a stupid story," Angela said. "The good brother

gets nothing for being good. The bad brother gets all the fun and just has to say sorry once."

"Yeah, but then he's *home*. For good. But that doesn't matter." He kept his eyes firmly on the greasy, greasy floor. "I *am* home."

"Oh, quit talking like a Pixar movie, dummy," she said, but she sat down next to him like she had that morning. He hadn't stopped shaking yet. "I could have picked a better day to tell you I was going away," she said.

"Nah, best to have it all at once."

"Is that true?"

"Probably not."

"You still want to go to the party?"

"I don't think I'm ready to go to my house yet."

"We could go to mine. You know my mom would totally be on your side."

"Can she send me to the Netherlands, too?"

"That would be awesome."

"But impossible."

They watched the cheese melt on the pizzas on the conveyor belt.

"So what *is* going to happen?" Angela asked, seriously. "You'll eventually have to go to them."

"I know. Will you come with me?"

"Absolutely. They like me. I'll be your human shield."

"But after that... I don't know. Christian school maybe."

"Your chances of getting laid would skyrocket."

"I don't know what else they'll do."

"Not gay cure therapy."

"I'll turn them in for child abuse if they try."

"*Some*one's feisty."

"It's been a rough day. And that's the thing, isn't it? They can be who they are and I can live with that and let them get on with it. But in return, I'm not going to put up with anything less."

"Damn straight, bubba." Then, more quietly, "Wouldn't it be amazing if that could happen?"

His phone buzzed again with another text from Marty. *Come home. Please.*

"At least they're distracted from the being-grandparents thing," Adam said.

"Big day for the Thorn family." Angela put her hand on his back. "Seriously, Adam. Are you safe there? They wouldn't hurt you. Not really. Would they?"

"I thought he was going to hit me today. In fact, I think I was hoping he would. It would have made him unambiguously the bad guy."

"He's not far off already."

"That's... Well, he's got his religion and it's important to him."

"And the moment it becomes more important than his kids, he's the bad guy."

"It's more complicated than that, Ange."

"No, it isn't." She stood, facing him again. "They're your parents. They're meant to love you *because*. Never *in spite*."

"That's your mom talking."

"My mom is a very wise woman." She went to the oven and put the last two finished pizzas in boxes. "If you're sure, I'll change clothes and we can get going."

"I'm sure."

She glanced at him. "I'm glad."

"What am I going to do without you, Angela?"

"Be okay." She shrugged. "That's a prediction and a demand." She couldn't conceal a grin. "And just think of all I'll be able to teach you when I get back."

"My murderer," the Queen says again.

The faun moves behind her. The man has pressed himself against the back wall, as far from the cell door as he can make himself go.

"Katie?" the man says. "Oh, God."

"You only see the one face?" the Queen asks.

"How can it be you? How can this be happening?"

"Silence," the Queen says, and the man is struck dumb, though his mouth still gulps air trying to form words.

But then, "Speak," she says, and the faun can hear the surprise in her voice.

"This is…" the man says. "This is some trick—"

"I have come to judge you," the Queen says.

And then she says, as if in contradiction of herself, "I have come to speak with you.

"I have come to kill you," she says.

"I have come to find out why," she says.

The faun is troubled, even more troubled than before. The two voices speak over each other, demanding different things. Have the worlds already begun to erupt over their borders?

"My Queen?" he asks again.

But she holds up the hand to silence him once more. "I will see this through," she says.

"But the world, my Queen."

"I will see this through."

She reaches forward, bending the bars of the cell as if they were so many reeds in the lake. The man gasps, but there is, of course, nowhere for him to run as the Queen steps into his presence.

Adam paid Emery for thirty-six pizzas, which even with Angela's staff discount came to nearly three hundred dollars.

"You don't *have* that much money," Angela said, as he refused to take any of hers.

"I said I'd get them." Adam picked up the first stack to take to his car. "The Garcias will pay me back."

"You aren't sure of that."

"I remain optimistic."

"Despite everything else that's happened today?"

"*Because* of it. How much worse can it get?"

"Oh, *dude*," Angela said, panicking, looking frantically around the back room at Pizza Frome Heaven to find some actual authentic wood to knock on. He took the pizzas out to his car; they were taking his rather than Angela's as it could hold more. His phone buzzed again as he put them in the back.

Marty. Again.

"For God's sake." Adam took a deep breath. "Hello?"

"Oh, praise God."

"Just 'hello' is fine, Marty."

"They've been worried sick."

"About what, I wonder?"

"That you'd do something to yourself."

"Do you really think this family is worth killing myself over?" Angela came out with the second stack of pizzas rising nearly to the level of her eyeballs. He helped her one-handedly put them next to the others.

"Adam–"

"What do you want, Marty?"

"You know what they want. For you to come home."

"No, not what *they* want. You. What do *you* want, Marty?"

He didn't answer at first, and Adam was ready to hang up, but then he said, "I want to feel safe."

"What?" Adam said, sounding so surprised, Angela looked up.

"Everything's..." Marty started. "Just sort of falling apart, isn't it?"

"What the hell are you talking about?"

Angela whispered to him, "Is everything okay?"

"I think Marty's lost his mind," he whispered back.

"Well," she said, "would that really be a surprise?"

"Are you there?" his brother asked.

"Yeah. What are you talking about, things falling apart?"

"Well, Dad's crying and Mom's really mad–"

"Neither of those things surprise me."

"And they're both talking about quitting the ministry."

This stopped Adam. But not for long. "That's an empty threat."

"I know–"

"They're trying to manipulate both of us."

"I *know*, Adam, I've lived with them longer than you have. I'm just saying, they're really upset."

"Upset isn't the same as the world falling apart."

"You haven't seen Dad's face."

Adam took a deep breath. "Yes, I did, Marty. I saw it when he suggested it was my own fault my boss touched me. I saw it when he tried to cast the devil out of me. When he told me all the conditions I needed to meet before I could be his son–"

"I don't believe he said that–"

"He didn't say anything like that when you told him about Felice?"

Marty was quiet.

"Marty, he told me that he had to *work* to love me." Adam took another breath. "And maybe he's right on that one."

"The *fuck* he is," Angela said, louder now.

"Angela's there?" Marty asked him.

"Marty, I'm going to go now. I'm not responsible for your life feeling safe. I might have been, once, if anyone there had cared–"

"It's *because* I care–"

"On your terms. No one else's."

"There are only God's terms."

"Goodbye, Marty–"

"Adam!" He said it loud enough to stop Adam, who just breathed into the phone, waiting for what his brother had to say. And what his brother ended up having to say was: "*I* love you, bro."

Adam's throat gripped, but he was angry that it did. "*Do* you, bro?"

"Without condition."

"I wish I could believe you, Marty."

"I know that they don't."

"What?"

"I know they don't. I see it with my own two eyes. Do you think I'm blind to how quickly they forgive me and how slow they are to forgive you? Today most of all."

"Why do either of us need to be forgiven so often?"

"It's … it's not Christian, what they're doing. How they're acting." Adam heard a car go by on the other end of the line. His brother must have gone outside to make the call. Wanted to make it away from their parents. "That's what I meant about things not feeling safe, Adam. They screamed about me and Felice but then they just... Opened their arms after your news. I was supposed to be on the same team as them. Against you."

"Marty–"

"I've committed my life to this. I'm not perfect, bro, far from it, but I know that love *can* be perfect. I just... I want you to know that *I* know I've been doing what they've been doing. For too long. I've put conditions on you. I've looked at you with pity."

"I know. It's been a carnival of delights."

"And I'm sorry for it, Adam. I can't say sorry enough. But my world isn't safe if I can't love my own brother. That's what it really felt like today. And that's not a world I can live in. So I love you, Adam. And whatever help you need from me to fix all this with Mom and Dad... Well, you got it."

Adam was silent again.

"You still there, bro?"

"Yeah."

"Maybe don't come home just now. Maybe let me talk to them. Maybe go to your party."

"It's just a get-together."

"Let me see what I can do. If anything."

"I'm not asking you to, Marty."

"You shouldn't have to. It should be what a brother does anyway. I should be protecting you. As much as I can."

"I'm not changing. I can't."

"As of today, bro, I'm no longer asking you to. Look, that's Mom coming out the front door. I'm assuming you don't want to talk to her?"

Adam heard "*Is that him?*" in the background of Marty's call.

"I really don't," he said.

"Take care of yourself, Adam," Marty said. "And remember I love you. I'm going to act a lot more like it from now on."

Marty hung up. Adam stared at his phone, like he'd just hung up on a call from outer space.

"What happened?" Angela asked.

"I don't even know."

"Are you going home?"

"No. Not yet."

"You choose your family, you know," she said. This was something she often said. Almost her mantra, especially as she came from the best-chosen family he'd ever met. "I chose you ages ago, Adam Thorn. Your family is here."

"I know it is," Adam said. "But maybe it just got one person bigger."

"How can it be you?" the man asks. He has urinated himself – the faun can smell it – and he seems to be trying to fold himself into the back corner of the cell in an effort to get away from her. "This is a nightmare. Something the screws are doing–"

"I will silence you again."

The man voluntarily closes his mouth, but the faun can still hear him whimpering.

"I have come…" the Queen starts to say, but then she stops. The faun waits, long enough that he can move around to see his Queen's face. With an astonishment that will accompany him through the rest of whatever brief eternity is to follow, he sees confusion there.

"My lady?" he says.

"I have come…" she says again. Then she looks into the face of the man, and she asks, "Why have I come, Tony?"

"You came to kill me," the man says.

The Queen's eyes focus on the man, clearer now. "Yes," she says. "That is what I came to do."

"I have come to kill you," she hears herself saying, and there is surety in it, a purity of purpose that is bracingly tart in her mouth, like a drink made from spring flowers. She will kill this man. She will make him pay for what he has done to her, for the bruises around her neck, for the mud in her lungs, for–

"Tony?" she says, and the clarity is gone.

There is a man in front of her, cowering in his corner. (There is another in the room, too, a man too large to be real, and she can only see him if she does not look directly at him.) But there is a man in front of her.

It's Tony.

"You murdered me," she says to him, and his eyes finally meet hers.

"You've come to drag me down to hell," he says.

"You murdered me," she says again.

"I didn't mean to–"

"You did."

"Only right that second," he says. "Only for a second."

"A second is all it takes."

"I've missed you so much."

She feels a flare of anger, and the short bed to her right catches fire. Tony cries out and shrinks back.

"You have no right to miss me," she says, and again

she feels her power, the other power that's there, the one giving her shape–

But no–

She calms, eyes still on the man, and the larger man she can only barely see pulls the burning mattress from the cell, extinguishing it.

"You have no right."

"I don't."

"You don't."

"What do you want from me, then?"

At this, she considers. And discovers she knows.

Adam pulled out of the parking lot and started the journey to the lake where the get-together was, the sun still hanging over the horizon, slowly making its way to set out past a sound, a peninsula and then into an ocean somewhere.

"Who's the rose for?" Angela said, picking it up from the floor.

"I got it this morning," Adam said. "Just felt right. Like I had to." He glanced over at her, thinking. "You know what? I thought it was a going-away thing for Enzo, then I wondered if it was for Linus, but I think it's gotta be for you. On this day. This going-away day for you, too."

Angela's face softened, she pushed out her lower lip, letting it quiver, and said, gently, "Do I fucking look like the kind of girl who wants flowers?" He laughed as she put it on the back seat. "*You're* that kind of girl, though," she said.

"You shouldn't use 'girl' as an insult."

"I'm reappropriating it."

"I see."

They drove in silence for a moment, then Angela said, "You won't vanish, will you?"

"What?"

"When I'm in Rotterdam. People always say they'll keep in touch, but then they find other friends and the times get less and less–"

"Skype every Wednesday and Saturday."

She nodded, solemnly. "If your parents let you have any sort of connection with the wider world."

"I'll go to your house and ask your mom."

She nodded again.

"We won't lose touch, Ange."

"It's college after," she said. "We might have lost touch anyway."

"We can deal with after, after. Let's get through the next thing first."

"That's a very mature attitude, Mr Thorn."

"One of us has to be, Ms Darlington." Adam glanced into his rear-view mirror, hearing sirens. He pulled over to let seven police cars speed by, going well over a hundred miles an hour, by the look of it. "Whoa. What's going on there?"

The cars all turned at the main intersection, towards the prison but away from the lake, so Adam figured he'd probably never know what it was about. Frome had already reached its annual quota of big news stories with the murder of Katherine van Leuwen.

Adam turned his car in the other direction, towards the paths where he ran lakeside, towards the nice cabin the Garcias had rented for their son's get-together.

"My stomach is actually starting to hurt," Adam said.

Angela sighed. "I'm so glad he's moving to Atlanta."

"I can't help how I feel. I can't help missing him."

"You know, everyone says that, but I wonder if it's actually true. If you tried hard enough."

"I can't help missing *you*."

"That's different. I'm supernatural."

Adam pulled his car up to the cabin. They weren't the first. At least half a dozen other cars were there, including—

"There's Linus," Angela said, nodding at him. He was already holding a cup of beer and seeing Adam pull in. Adam parked, and he and Angela got out, ready to go.

But then a voice said, "Pizza's here!" and Adam saw Enzo approaching with a smile and his heart broke, it broke, it broke.

They are indoors, in a room, a corridor, with no windows of any kind, yet the faun knows how close they're getting to sunset. Time is running out. And then all of time will run out. He has known it as a thought since this morning, since following the Queen out of the lake, but it is only now, this close, that he begins to feel real fear.

They will not make it.

She nears the man, looking him up and down. She reaches out to touch him, but before her fingers land, he flinches away, hitting his head hard on the metal wall. She can sense the bruise forming below the skin, the smaller bruise forming on his brain, and with a wave of her fingers, she heals it, almost without a thought.

"Am I dead?" the man asks.

•   •   •

"You should be so lucky," the Queen says, and the colloquialism of it tells the faun the other spirit is in charge here. The one who cannot hear him. The one completely unaware of the danger.

She touches the man on his elbow, the nearest bit of flesh to her. It burns so fast, the faun can smell it cook. The ancient urge is awakened, the forbidden one: the faun grows hungry.

The man calls out and falls to the floor in the corner of his cell. The Queen stands over him.

And the faun can feel her indecision.

"Why are you so afraid?" she says to the man, feeling real bafflement. This is Tony. Tony who knew her. Tony who killed her. Tony should be frightened, yes, but this cowering, this abjectness...

"You've come to kill me," Tony weeps.

"How can I kill you if you think you're already dead?" she answers. "Were you always this foolish?"

"Yes," Tony answers, almost immediately.

And there. The power of a word. The power of one word. That's where it all changes.

"Hey, Adam," Enzo said, hugging him. For that instant and that instant alone, Adam was holding him again, inhaling the smell of Enzo's hair, dark and wavy and so thick it almost seemed alien compared to Adam's destined-to-thin blondness.

Then Enzo was pulling away. Maybe for the last time ever. And if Adam had mostly made his peace with this, "mostly" was as close to "not at all" as any hand grenade.

"Glad you came," Enzo said. "Hey, Angela!"

"Whatever," Angela said, unloading the pizzas.

Enzo smiled to himself. "I suppose it's too late to ever heal that friendship." He looked up in Adam's eyes. "But I'm glad you're here."

"Yeah, Enzo," Adam said, thinking, I love you, I love you–

Then a mutinous thought: was he only thinking that because Enzo expected him to?

Where had *that* come from?

"You look well," Enzo said. "Feels like I haven't seen you all summer."

"You haven't."

Enzo looked surprised. "Really?"

"We keep missing each other."

Enzo made a face. "I just kind of thought you were hanging out with Linus."

"Doesn't mean you and I couldn't have hung out, too."

Enzo gave him a look, trying to guess what Adam meant. Adam couldn't have told him; he didn't know either. But here was Enzo. Here was the face he had been so close to. Here was the body he knew so well. The touch and the smell and the taste of it. Here was the mouth that had hinted at so many wonderful things while saying so few wonderful things straight out. Here was the mouth that broke his heart.

And maybe, Adam thought, maybe hearts don't ever stop breaking once broken. Maybe they just keep on beating, until they're broken again, and then they keep on beating still. His heart was broken just at the sight of Enzo, it *longed* to touch him again, even after all that Enzo had done.

But it still beat. And a part of it was wondering where Linus had got to, because that broken heart had leapt a little when he saw Linus standing there.

"Anyway," Enzo said, breaking a silence that had become uncomfortable.

"I'm going to miss you, Enzo," Adam said, meaning it.

"Angela's going away, too, for all of senior year."

"Really?" Enzo said, sounding genuinely concerned.

"It's okay. We'll keep in touch."

"*We* will, too."

"Sure, Enzo."

Adam paused, trying to put his finger on what seemed odd here. Then he realized there was something troubling about the physical *fact* of Enzo–

He was somehow *smaller* than Adam remembered. Still bigger than Linus, but smaller, too. Out of nowhere, Adam thought of the night he and Enzo had first argued. Whenever he told the story to anyone else, he would always say he couldn't remember what it was over, but that was a lie: it was because Enzo had been jealous. *Enzo*. He'd seen Adam laughing with a guy from the cross-country team and on the basis of nothing at all, accused Adam of sleeping around.

The argument had been fairly quickly settled – there was neither evidence nor intention and Enzo had apologized – but what Adam remembered, what he *always* remembered, was how big Enzo had seemed. Not physically, no one was ever really going to tower over Adam, but that first Enzo's anger, then the astonishment that Adam felt that Enzo felt jealous over *him*, had filled up the room, filled up everything.

That anger had seemed so large that, for a moment, all of Adam's future depended on the outcome. Until it was settled, even though he wasn't in the wrong, Adam felt his life teetering. What if he lost him? What if he lost

Enzo? It would be the end of the world. It would be the end of all hope. And that Enzo seemed, implicit behind all the jealousy, to feel the same, well, that just made him bigger and bigger until he took up every corner of Adam's potential oxygen.

But then that world *did* end, didn't it?

And now, here was Enzo. Just another of the many humans shorter than Adam.

When did that happen?

"Anyway," Enzo said again.

Adam looked at him, but Enzo wouldn't meet his eye any more, clearly wanting this to be over. "You know what?" Adam started–

But never finished because two things happened and it all changed. The first was larger on the surface, but the second was the one that actually did it.

The first was that a big, strawberry-blonde girl came over from the tables where Angela and Linus and other people including JD McLaren from the garden centre and Renee and Karen from Adam's work were digging into the pizzas. Adam didn't recognize the girl, but she put her arm around Enzo's shoulders, he turned his face to her and they kissed. They kissed right there in front of Adam.

"Hey," the girl said, really friendly. "I'm Natasha. Nat."

Adam shook her hand. "Adam."

"*You're* Adam?" Nat said, smiling wide. "Enzo talks about you all the time."

Adam looked at Enzo, but Enzo looked away. "We were good friends in school is all," Enzo said.

Still stunned, Adam asked, "Where did you two–"

"Summer job in his mom's office," Nat said. "Though I don't think his parents approve because I'm not very Latina."

"You're not at all Latina," Enzo said.

"Hey, my family came over on the *Mayflower*. I could be *anything* by now." She smiled again at Adam, comfortable with the silence. Her face brightened. "You brought all those pizzas, didn't you?"

"Yeah," Adam said.

"That was really cool of you."

"Thanks."

"That reminds me," Enzo said, and he took out his wallet. And this was the second thing. So much smaller than Enzo suddenly having a girlfriend, so much smaller than the walking, talking evidence that Enzo had moved on (certainly smaller than the ground-heaving possibility that Adam might have moved on a little bit as well), but this was the moment where it all changed. This strange small moment. Adam would even be able to put his finger on it in all the years to come. The power of one action.

"Will a hundred and fifty cover it?" Enzo asked, holding out cash.

Adam just stared at it for a minute, and his heart broke in a different way. A way that felt suddenly, terrifyingly free.

"That's okay," he heard himself saying. "A going-away present."

Enzo grinned, surprised. "Thanks, Adam."

"Yeah," was all Adam could say back.

"Can I get you a beer?" Nat said.

"Nah, I'm fine," Adam said. "I can get my own."

He turned back to the even larger group of people now, the group gathered to say farewell to Enzo, and now that Adam had done that himself, he was suddenly desperate to find Linus, hoping in an increasing panic that he hadn't ruined everything.

"I was always this much of an idiot," Tony says, still weeping. "One stupid thing after another."

"And I'm supposed to feel sorry for you?"

"No!" he practically wails. "I'm just saying that I deserve it!"

"Deserve what?"

He looks at her, fear and – the faun is surprised to see – a kind of relief in his eyes. He can tell by the Queen's face that she sees it, too.

Sees it and is displeased.

"Is that what you think this is?" she says to him. "Your release?"

"Isn't it?" he asks.

"I came here to tell you what I know. If you are released by it, then I have failed."

She touches his skin again, the sizzle of the burn

lasting only an instant but he collapses. He is a bug, she realizes. Nothing more than a bug to be stepped on—

No.

No, she also thinks. No, more than that. I will tell him.

"I will tell you," she says. "Are you listening?"

He looks up at her, wounded now, chastened. "I am."

She tells him.

"I was alive when you took your hands off me," the faun hears her say. "I was alive when your fingers left their bruises on my neck."

There is a different kind of fear on the man's face now. The fear of waking up from a dream into something much worse.

"No," Tony says.

"I was alive when you wept over me. I was alive when you lifted my body from the floor. I was alive when you found bricks to put in my pockets—"

"No. Nonononono—"

"I was alive when you put me in the lake, Tony." She kneels to him. "I was still alive."

"You can't be... I checked—"

"You didn't check closely enough. You were too high, too far gone—"

There is a surprising surge of terrified defiance on his face, and he shouts at her, "So were you!"

•   •   •

Before she can even think, she removes his head from his body.

The faun can't fix this, not while the Queen still holds the man's head. But perhaps this is what the spirit bound to her needed. It seems the most obvious, this straight revenge, this violent act to match the one that robbed the spirit of her body–

Except–

Except that isn't what he feels in the spirit. Her spirit is questing, searching, lost. This isn't the action of the spirit.

This is the action of a Queen.

And then she or the Queen or the hybrid that the two have become, that changing, shifting personality that the faun must somehow unravel, that voice says:

"No."

"Where'd Linus go?" he asked Angela.

"Bathroom," she answered, surprisingly curt.

"That bad?"

"You ignored him the second Enzo spoke a syllable. Not your best move, Wild Thornberry."

"Shit," he said. "And I just… Angela, I think I just *got* it with Enzo."

"*Now?* A little late, isn't it?"

"That was his girlfriend."

Angela spat out half a mouthful of beer right onto the dusty ground. "His what?"

"I know."

"No, seriously, his *what?*"

"Maybe he's bi. Or fluid. Like you."

She gave him a look that said comparing her and Enzo was an endeavour embarked upon by fools. She looked around until she found Nat in the ever-growing crowd of partygoers. "Oh, my God," Angela said. "She looks like *you*."

"What? No, she…" But he stopped. "Oh, wow."

"That's probably the weirdest compliment you're ever going to get."

"But, no, Angela, this isn't the important thing. The important thing is he offered to pay me for the pizzas. Not even close to enough either."

Her eyebrows rose in confusion. "What?"

"I'll explain but I need to find Linus first."

"Yeah, you do."

"Don't go anywhere?"

She took the flesh of his upper arm between two fingers and gently pinched. "Not even when I'm across a continent and an ocean," she said.

"Not even then," he agreed.

"Not even until the end of the world."

He set off to find Linus, but only got to the other end of the little campground before Karen and Renee stopped him. "What happened with you and Wade?" Karen asked. "You ran out of there like he tried to kiss you."

She meant this as a joke, but when Adam didn't answer, Renee said, "He *didn't*."

"He did. When I said I wouldn't sleep with him, he fired me." Adam blinked. Was it as clear as that? Maybe it was. Maybe it really was.

"He can't do that," Renee said, concern all over her face.

"He really can't," Karen agreed.

"We're backing you up," Renee suddenly said, which surprised him as he always thought of Karen as the more take-charge one.

"Hell, yeah, we are," Karen said. "How *dare* he?"

"Are you going to talk to Mitchell?" Renee said.

Mitchell was their regional manager, a man Adam had never even spoken to. "I've never even spoken to him."

"He goes to our church," Karen said. "He's a good guy. You should talk to him."

"We'll back you up," Renee said again.

"You didn't see it, though."

"Please," Karen said, "all the stuff Wade has said while we worked there? The way he looks at you?"

"The way he always touches you?" Renee said, softly.

"You guys noticed that?" Adam said, honestly amazed.

"Impossible to miss, Adam," Karen said. "We always wondered how bad you needed the job to put up with it."

He felt a little knot in his stomach. "I need the job pretty bad."

"Then you'll get it back," Renee said. "No way I'm working there if Wade's there and you're not."

"This isn't over, Adam," Karen said. "No way, no how."

"Well, that's…" Adam said. "That's kind of amazing. Thank you."

"You're welcome." Renee smiled, shy again.

"Now, really, have you seen Linus?"

"I think he went out on one of the paths by the lake," Karen said. "Why?"

He looked her right in the eye and said, "I have to give him a rose."

"No," she says, and the rebuke is not for the faun, nor is it for the dead man whose head she still holds, whose blood spreads across the floor of the cell, a brook overflowing its bank.

"No," she says again.

In an instant, the man is whole again, cowering back in the corner, his blood running through his veins, though the smell lingers, a smell still churning the ferocious hunger in the faun's belly. It has been so long–

And then he realizes. These desires, this hunger, this is because his Queen really is slipping away.

"No," she says, as the man looks back up at her, the shock in his eyes not lessening. She has allowed him to retain the memory of the beheading, to remember the pain, the feeling of separation. It would normally tip his mind beyond reach, but she disallows that.

He will remember. He will always remember.

And that's enough.

A part of her feels that the beheading was only right, but the larger part, the part that drove her here, that part knows his death would be only the most callow of revenge. It's what she learned the moment he said yes. The moment where everything changed.

It had taken pushing beyond that to realize its folly.

"You are so small," she says to him. "So ... puny."

He goggles back at her, mystified at what she will do next. She doesn't know that either.

"I came here to tell you of my murder," she says, "and then to kill you, but you..." She steps back from the man. "You are so small."

The faun does not know who is speaking now. He doubts she does either.

"There is more here," she says, feeling it as she says it. "You loved me."

"I did," the man says, simply.

"But you loved the drugs more."

"Everyone does."

She nods at the simple truth of this. "I loved you, once."

"I know."

"Even when I loved the drugs more, I would not have done what you did."

"I'm weaker than you."

"You are. Everyone is. Do you know the responsibility of that?"

"No," the man says.

"And for that, this world rejoices."

She turns to the faun, looks in his eye, and says, "I am lost."

Adam found Linus on a little promontory looking out over the lake, across the inlet from the path he'd run what felt like a hundred years ago but was actually just this morning. Linus had a beer in his hand, watching the sun dip low in the sky.

"Hey," he said, seemingly cheerfully as Adam came up. "Is that for me?"

Adam held the rose in his hand. He'd gone back to his car to get it.

"Will you take it?" Adam said.

Linus looked up and said, plainly, without malice, "No."

"Linus–"

"I tried for you, Adam. I really, really did."

"Linus, I know–"

"I don't think you do. You're not the easiest guy in the world, you know."

Adam faltered, that knot in his stomach again. "What do you mean?"

Linus made a rushing motion with his hands on either side of Adam's head, spilling a little beer on Adam's shirt. "All this stuff," Linus said, "always going on. Always the world tumbling down on you. Always you trying to hold it all up." He sipped his beer and said, more quietly, "It's no wonder you only notice the guys who treat you badly."

Adam swallowed and turned the rose in his hands, turned it round and round. "The pizzas," he said. "The pizzas were meant to be a last gift to Enzo before he moved away. He didn't say as much but that's what we both meant."

"Yeah, I got that. Look, Adam–"

"He tried to pay me for them."

Linus hesitated, clearly not sure where this was going.

"That's how he sees me," Adam said. "I hoped and hoped and hoped. For *a year and a half*. And then he dumped me. For the worst, stupidest reasons. And I guess… I guess I still hoped. Even when I knew I shouldn't. Even when I had better things right in front of me." He looked over at Linus. "He was the first way out for me. The first way out of all the rest of this stuff that races and races. The first window to a world that *could* be, a world I'm kind of desperate for. And he had my heart, I admit that."

"That much was obvious, Adam. To anyone who looked."

"But he tried to pay me for the pizzas. He wouldn't even let me be generous. Which I think is what I was secretly hoping for all this time. He didn't calculate it or anything. There was just … no connection left for him there." He turned the rose again. "Whatever I was before, I'm now just a guy who did him a favour he needed to repay."

Linus eyed him. "That must have hurt."

"Who cares, Linus? Who *cares*? It woke me up. I've... God, do you know how little I think I have? How much I think goes wrong for me? With my parents and work and Angela moving away?"

"But that's all true, kinda," Linus said, gently. "Don't pretend things aren't–"

"Yeah, but they're not the only things that are true. There's so much more that's also true." He still turned the rose around and around. "You sure you won't take this?"

"Feels like it's kind of overweighted with meaning now. That's an awful lot to put on one rose."

"Probably."

"Here's the thing, Adam. I know what I want. Not all of it, but the right amount. I want you, but not at any price. I want to get through my senior year with friends and I want you to be one of them and I want you lying in my bed and I want you naked in my shower and I want us to laugh and I want you to actually be there. All of you. Not seventy per cent with the rest still wondering if Enzo is ever going to come back after burrowing so far into the closet it's like he's looking for straight Narnia."

Adam laughed a little at this, but Linus's face continued serious. "Do you know what you want, Adam?" he asked. "You want out, I know that, but there are lots of ways out. Do you just want that one?"

He waited. Adam still spun the rose, the rose that seemed destined now to be given to no one, the rose bought on the spur of the moment after he'd pricked his thumb. He put a thorn back to the wound again, idly pricking himself once more, just wanting to feel the pain for a second–

–and saw it again, an entire world, fast as a gasped breath, of trees and green, of water and woods, of a figure that followed, dark, in the background, of mistakes made, of loss, of grief, of a world ending, ending, ending–

He blinked and put his bloody thumb to his lips like he had at the beginning of this eternal, pivotal day. Here at the end of it, there was only the coppery taste of blood on his tongue.

He knew what to say.

"I want to take you back to the party, Linus," he said, low, like he was asking for a permission he was terrified of not getting. "I want to kiss you in front of everyone there. I want everyone to know." Raising his eyes to look directly into Linus's face was maybe the scariest thing he'd had to do all day long, but it was only the free-falling terror that always accompanied hope.

"I want to love you," Adam said. "If you'll let me."

"I do not know how to let her go," the Queen says, directly to the faun, and this, too, shows the terrifying diminution of her power. Not just admitting to a lack of knowledge, but the implicit request to an underling of the court for help.

"Does she know how to let you go, my lady?" he asks, trying to stay calm. "It was her spirit who first caught yours."

"It was not," the Queen says, as if admitting an embarrassment. "I saw her there. I was curious. There was a loss, an unanswered question. And now—"

"The binds of the world are coming loose, my lady. We have until the sun sets. That's all the time given to a spirit to wander. You know this. She will die, and if you die with her—"

"We are too entwined." There is fear in her voice now, and this shakes the faun more than any of the other cataclysms this day has contained. "I do not know where she ends and I begin."

275

"Time will finish, my lady. This world—"

"This world's walls will dissolve. And this world along with it."

"And ours."

She looks up to him, a regal set to her jaw that gives him hope, a resignation in her eyes that contradicts this—

—and there is a moment where she seems to vanish, to become as insubstantial as a breath of air, and she sees their home again, not just the lake, but this world entire, all the souls beating within it, all the longings and the lonelinesses, the spirit wrapped to her, the spirits who circle out from that one, the spirits spinning out from those and beyond and beyond and beyond, this world that thrums with a life constantly consuming itself and regenerating anew, this world she has been Queen of since before the memories of all but herself, she sees it all, past and forever, every soul that lives and could, the ones she killed, the ones she saved, and this soul, this soul, this spirit bound to her and of her and with her and in her, this spirit who pardoned her own murderer, this spirit who said no to that chain of destruction these creatures so regularly set themselves upon, and at the end, she sees herself, all of herself, in a single drop of blood, a single drop of blood on a day where destinies changed, a single drop of blood that started this all—

•   •   •

–she knows what to do. The only option left to her.

"Let us return to our home," she says, certain that this is right. "Let us greet the end there."

"My Queen–"

"I am your Queen," she agrees. "And this is my wish."

Time is so short that for a vertiginous moment, the faun considers arguing with her, demanding that she try harder, try to see all that is at stake–

"Will you take my hand?" she asks.

An offer never made in all the eternities he has served her.

It really is the end.

"Yes, my lady," he says. "Let us return to our world and greet the end there."

He takes her hand.

8

RELEASE

"So what's going to happen?" Angela said, as they dipped their feet into the lake at the end of a small pier the party had expanded to accommodate.

"Always a million-dollar question," Linus said on the other side of Adam. Little fish darted around in the frankly freezing water, even in late August. Frome wasn't a town where a lot of open-air swimming got done.

"Which part?" Adam said. He was still holding the rose, had held it when he kissed Linus in the middle of the party, held it when the party kept spinning and the world didn't end. He hadn't even tried to catch Enzo's eye, and that felt right, too.

"With your parents first," Angela said. "You can always stay with mine if things get black. Always."

"I know," Adam said. "And I might. I'll have to see. Maybe Marty will keep his word and be on my side."

"Maybe he got an eyeful of what being the Prodigal Son actually looks like," Linus said.

"But you've always got a place," Angela repeated. "I mean it."

"I know. Thanks."

"What about the rest?" Linus asked.

"Well," Adam said. "What have I got? I've got a few hours until I have to go home and face that mess. I've got a few days until I'm supposed to go back to work if I'm not fired. And I've got a week before Angela goes to Europe. Those aren't the worst slots of time to live in, are they?"

"How about right now?" Linus said, nodding at the sun, setting on the horizon in front of them. "We've got a few minutes until the sun goes down."

"And this day is over," Adam said.

"And something new can begin?" Angela said, sceptical. "Am I the only one here who doesn't live in a Mickey Mouse Club song?"

"Sometimes, Ange," Adam said, "you just got to eat the corn and enjoy it." He pulled his feet out of the water and stood up between them. "Anyone want anything? Cold pizza? More beer?"

"I kinda want a water," Angela said.

"That sounds good," Linus agreed.

"Look at us," Adam said. "Teen party animals."

"I think we're pretty typical," Angela said, nodding back to the party. Adam looked, too. Small groups of people talking, an odd sense of relief gently misting through everyone that the party was a friendly one, no one going over the top, or at least not in any way that

282

didn't seem right. He saw Renee and Karen talking to JD McLaren and laughing in an unguarded way. Enzo, in fact, was the only one who'd drunk too much and was looking miserable next to Nat as she, possibly with purposeful obliviousness, laughed with what Adam guessed were friends of hers.

"Wow," Linus said, also looking. "Am I the only one who thinks Enzo's new girlfriend–"

"I know," Angela said. "Creepy, huh?"

Linus shrugged. "Maybe he's just lost. Maybe we should feel sorry for him."

"Or maybe he's a liar and a coward," Angela said.

"I don't even know," Adam said. "And I'm kind of okay with that."

He started walking back down the pier to get his friends some water.

"Hey," Angela called after him. "You coming back?"

He turned to them and smiled. "Always," he said. "Until the end of the world."

The faun leads her to the water. Her hand feels warm, soft, like a human hand, not the hand of his Queen, yet it is indubitably that as well. He can feel the power of her, even entwined in the spirit.

They reach the water's edge. She hesitates.

"This is where I left the lake," she says.

"I know, my Queen."

"This is where I began to die."

"Not all of you."

She looks him in the eye. "This is where I shall die now."

He has no answer for that. She still holds his hand. "The spirit wishes to leave me. She does not know how. I do not know how to release her. We are bound."

She looks to him, seeing him, her servant since time immemorial. She peers beyond his eyes, past the shape of the faun, to the spirit-shape that has always attended her.

"You have followed me," she says. "You have been at my side even when I couldn't see you."

"Yes, my Queen."

"You followed me when I was not your Queen."

"My Queen was always there. I followed her, as is my duty. And my will."

"Your will."

"Yes, my Queen."

She regards the hand she still holds. "You searched for me when I was lost."

"A Queen is never lost. She is always exactly where she needs to be."

She glances up at this and he can see a glimmer of the playful smile every Queen holds in reserve, the smile that is the doorway to her private self, the one who wears the role of Queen.

He feels a pressure on his hand and is astonished to realize she is pulling him closer, compounding the crime of contact with one of a proximity no spirit is ever allowed. "Is it not a shame," she says, "that we must wait until the end of the world for all boundaries to fall?"

"My Queen?" he asks, for the desire to move into her embrace is overwhelming to the point of extinguishment. He will perish there, but the perishing will be a bliss he has never even—

"Oh, hello," says a voice. "I didn't know anyone was on these paths."

They look over. A human creature, man-sized, the faun notes, but not perhaps all the way to being a man just yet. Close, though. Very close indeed.

The Queen no longer looks like the Queen. She looks again like the girl who rose out of the lake, the one put there still alive, the one that reached out in confusion and bound his Queen to her, to the doom of the world entire.

The boy frowns. "Do I know you?"

And then the spirit, not the Queen, but the spirit herself reaches out and asks of the boy, simply, "How do I let go?"

The boy pauses, surprised. His eyes flit to the faun, accepting him simply, with a glance, as the sun makes its first kiss of the horizon. The doom begins. The doom begins but—

"That's the question, isn't it?" says the boy. "For everyone."

"Everyone," the spirit agrees.

The boy takes a breath. "Today was a day I had to let go of a lot of stuff. Like everything that was tying me down suddenly got untied."

"And I the same," the spirit says. "Today is the day my destiny changed."

285

"So did mine."

"I know," the spirit says. "I heard it coming. I followed the longing for it."

She looks at the rose he twirls in his hand. There is one thorn that he idly pricks at with his thumb, and the faun can feel the Queen's thumb move in kind. The boy looks up to her again.

"I think I know who you are," he says.

"How do I let go?" the spirit merely asks again.

"I don't know," the boy says, "but I think this is for you."

He holds out the rose.

And the spirit steps away from the Queen to take it.

It is, in the end, that simple.

"Oh," says the spirit, with a surprised laugh. "Yes. I have found my release…"

Her words and continued laughter surround them as a breeze, turning petals of a rose on it, twisting and spiralling, until finally fading to nothing as the spirit makes her final passage, leaving only a scent of late summer in her wake, as if the world has let out a sigh, one of relief, one of renewal, and carries on spinning.

"Well," says the boy, "that was weird."

He gives one last look to the place where the faun stands, then back out to the setting sun, now halfway down. "I have found my release," he whispers to himself. "Into what, though?"

But then he smiles. He turns and, hands in his pockets, leaves the faun there, at the water's edge. The faun feels a tremendous freedom as his physical form dissipates, moving once more into pure spirit, into a world saved, a world released. He feels her beside him, feels the warmth of her happiness at her freedom and the continuing surprising warmth of her regard. The embrace still awaits him. Perhaps it won't extinguish him. Perhaps the freedom can arrive before the world itself ends.

He will find out. Whatever happens next, he will find out. His spirit turns to hers, open and willing to follow wherever she may lead.

"My Queen," he says. For there she is.

Notes & Acknowledgements

The name Angela Darlington was won at auction to raise money for Diversity Role Models, a charity which tackles homophobia in schools and of which I am a patron. Find out more about their amazing work on www.diversityrolemodels.org. I thank the real Angela Darlington and hasten to add that the resemblance ends at her name. This is a work of fiction. My own father, for example, is not in these pages.

Thanks to my agent and friend Michelle Kass and my editors Denise Johnstone-Burt at Walker and Rosemary Brosnan at HarperCollins for never once baulking at the zigzag sequence of books I keep turning in.

The spirit of Virginia Woolf's *Mrs Dalloway* and Judy Blume's *Forever* suffuse *Release*. I can only encourage you to read both to see where I've fallen short.